UNDER
AMELIA'S
WING

UNDER AMELIA'S WING

BOOK 2 *of the*
GINNY ROSS Series

—◆—

HEATHER STEMP

NIMBUS
PUBLISHING
— NIMBUS.CA —

Nimbus Publishing Limited
3660 Strawberry Hill St, Halifax, NS, B3K 5A9
(902) 455-4286 nimbus.ca

Printed and bound in Canada
NB1451

This story is a work of fiction, inspired by a true story. Names, characters, incidents, and places, including organizations and institutions, either are the product of the author's imagination or are used fictitiously.

Cover design: Colin Smith
Interior design: Heather Bryan
Editor: Emily MacKinnon
Cover and interior photos: Purdue University Archives

Library and Archives Canada Cataloguing in Publication

Title: Under Amelia's Wing / Heather Stemp.
Names: Stemp, Heather, 1945- author.
   Description: Series statement: Ginny Ross series ; book 2
   Identifiers: Canadiana (print) 2020015933X | Canadiana (ebook) 20200160524 | ISBN 9781771088503 (softcover) | ISBN 9781771088510 (HTML)
Classification: LCC PS8637.T46 U53 2020 | DDC jC813/.6—dc23

Nimbus Publishing acknowledges the financial support for its publishing activities from the Government of Canada, the Canada Council for the Arts, and from the Province of Nova Scotia. We are pleased to work in partnership with the Province of Nova Scotia to develop and promote our creative industries for the benefit of all Nova Scotians.

For
Llewellyn Crane
1932–2018
and
William James (Jim) Ross
1950–2017

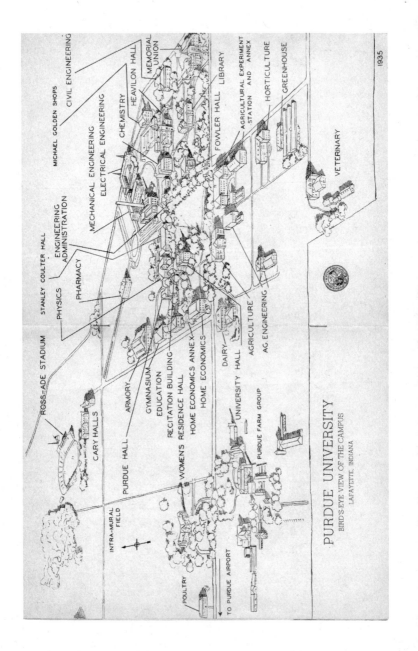

ROSS–ADE STADIUM

CARY HALLS

INTRA-MURAL FIELD

PURDUE HALL

WOMEN'S RESIDENCE HALL

TO PURDUE AIRPORT

POULTRY

MICHAEL GOLDEN SHOPS

CIVIL ENGINEERING

STANLEY COULTER HALL

ENGINEERING ADMINISTRATION

MECHANICAL ENGINEERING

ELECTRICAL ENGINEERING

CHEMISTRY

HEAVILON HALL

MEMORIAL UNION

PHYSICS

PHARMACY

FOWLER HALL

LIBRARY

AGRICULTURAL EXPERIMENT STATION AND ANNEX

HORTICULTURE

GREENHOUSE

ARMORY

GYMNASIUM

EDUCATION

RECITATION BUILDING

HOME ECONOMICS ANNEX

HOME ECONOMICS

DAIRY

AGRICULTURE

AG. ENGINEERING

UNIVERSITY HALL

PURDUE FARM GROUP

VETERINARY

1935

PURDUE UNIVERSITY

BIRD'S-EYE VIEW OF THE CAMPUS

LAFAYETTE, INDIANA

CONTENTS

1. Lafayette, Indiana 1

2. Purdue University 11

3. Airport 18

4. Registration 27

5. Taylor Cub 34

6. Professor Jones 43

7. New Friends 49

8. Old Friend 56

9. Amelia 62

10. Atlantic Flight 68

11. Truth 75

12. Convocation 85

13. Choices 95

14. Change 103

15. Goodbye 111

16. Promise 117

17. Football 122

18. Good News 126

19. Christmas 134

20. New Year's Eve 142

21. Marks 150

22. Last Resort 156

23. Letter 162

24. Worn Out 167

25. *News* 172

26. *At Last* 178

27. *Set Back* 183

28. *Not Alone* 190

29. *New Route* 197

30. *Howland Island* 208

31. *Recovery* 215

32. *Moving On* 220

33. *Ground School* 224

34. *Flight* 229

35. *June 1940* 236

36. *Goodbye* 242

Photos 248

Author's Note 251

Acknowledgements 253

CHAPTER ONE

LAFAYETTE, INDIANA

AUGUST 1936

———◄○►———

I T WAS SOME hot on the railway platform. Not Newfoundland hot, where a cool breeze always blew in from the bay. This was a still, white hot. Leaves wilted on the trees and cicadas buzzed loudly. Not a hill, rock face, or body of water broke the expanse of train tracks and soot-covered red brick buildings.

Behind me stood the station. I glanced at my trunk and decided it would be safe for a few minutes. I walked into the waiting room, then checked the bathroom. Both were empty. The door to the stationmaster's office was locked. I knocked but there was no answer. Butterflies started swirling in my stomach. Where were the other students? Where were the taxis?

Back on the platform, I rubbed my hands together and paced. The university expected me today. That was what I had told them in my telegram. I wiped my forehead with the back of my hand and tried to think.

I'd travelled alone before, but this was different. Very few people from my hometown of Harbour Grace, Newfoundland, went to university, and when they did, it was to McGill in Montreal. I didn't know what to expect at Purdue, and if I got lonely, there was no money to go home in the summers.

In truth, I was worried about being away from my family for four years. They needed me. I'd been the only one bringing in a salary. Dad had tried to run our family grocery store after Papa died, but he just didn't have it in him. Where Papa was friendly and outgoing, Dad was quiet and shy. So instead, Dad was in Toronto looking for work. The problem was he never seemed to make enough money to send some home.

Mom and Nana still traded sewing and knitting for food they couldn't grow themselves, but they needed money to pay for coal and electricity. When I left, my brother Billy said he'd take over my kitchen duties at our Aunt Rose's hotel, but he was only twelve years old. For him, there was still the question of what would win out—earning money for the family, or fishing with his friends.

I walked to the edge of the platform and looked in both directions. Nothing but empty tracks and heat that was making me feel right woozy. I had to get out of the sun and figure out what to do next.

The only shade was next to the station, so I pulled my trunk against the wall and sat down. I took my acceptance letter out of my pocket and unfolded it. Maybe I'd missed some detail that could help me get to the university.

Virginia Ross
22 Water Street
Harbour Grace, Newfoundland

June 10, 1936

Dear Miss Ross,

On behalf of the faculty and staff at Purdue University, I am pleased to congratulate you on your acceptance to our Engineering program. You are currently enrolled in Mechanical Engineering where you will spend two years. At the end of that time you may choose to specialize in Aeronautical Engineering for another two years. This will qualify you to graduate with a degree and a pilot's license.

The president of the University, Dr. Edward C. Elliott, has a mandate to attract women into higher education at Purdue. To this end, he has hired Amelia Earhart as a part-time career counsellor for women and an aviation advisor. I know she will be very interested in working with a student with your interest and experience.

Please find enclosed all the necessary enrollment forms. We would appreciate receiving them by August 15, 1936, in order to confirm your place in our fall program. Since you will be arriving from out of country, please inform us of your arrival date so we may be on hand to welcome you to our campus.

If you have any questions or problems, please do not hesitate to contact us.

Yours sincerely,

Klazina McKeigan

Admissions Department

Purdue University

I jumped to my feet. "I most certainly do have a problem!" I shouted. "How do I get to the university?"

I waited a few seconds for a reply, hoping some railway worker in a nearby building had heard me. The cicadas buzzed loudly but there was no other sound.

I folded the letter and put it in my pocket. The butterflies started swirling in my stomach again. I walked back into the waiting room and rattled the doorknob of the stationmaster's office. Still locked.

I was heading out the door when I thought I heard a sound. I froze and listened. Then I ran to the edge of the platform and peered down the tracks. Still nothing but hot, shimmering air in both directions.

I started pacing again. Even if there were no taxis, there should be a bus running between the station and the university. But where was the stop? And if I left the platform to look for it, would my trunk be safe?

I folded my arms over the top of my head and continued pacing, until I heard it again. A sound so far off that I couldn't be sure what it was. I frowned and listened. I wanted to believe it was a train whistle but it could easily have been the call of a bird or the cry of an animal off in the distance. I checked the tracks again. Nothing.

I'd been travelling for six days; the university expected me today, and I was stuck at the train station. Tears of frustration pooled in my eyes. I pulled out the handkerchief Mom had embroidered for me as a going-away present and dabbed my eyes. Then I held it over my nose and inhaled the scent of her lavender powder. I walked back to my trunk and sat down in the shade.

With my finger, I traced the small blue forget-me-nots and the message Mom had stitched in the corner of the hanky: *We're so proud of you.* I smiled at the sentiment, knowing it hadn't always been like that. The message had almost been, *Over my dead body.* That's what Mom said whenever I made the mistake of mentioning aviation in front of her.

Convincing her I was capable of becoming a pilot took a long time. In the end, it was Amelia Earhart's transatlantic flight from Harbour Grace that paved my way. I remember the day Mom and I had our showdown. She had been standing behind the long counter in the store when I walked in. Before I could open my mouth she said, "If you're going to talk about being a pilot, you can turn around and walk straight out that door!" She pointed to the door to emphasize her message.

She'd always been a pointer and a slapper, so I kept my distance while I tried to think of what to say next. I decided to get the issue out on the table.

"Why don't you want me to be a pilot?"

She had given me all kinds of reasons that illustrated my lack of skill in most things she considered important. "If you can't hem a skirt, Ginny, how can you fly a plane?"

"You hit the nail on the head," I'd shot back. "Flying is probably the only way I'll be successful."

We'd gone back and forth for some minutes before we got to the crux of the matter. She loved me and was afraid of losing me. At last, I had what eluded me all my life—my mother's love and concern instead of her embarrassment over my shortcomings.

One more deep breath into Mom's hanky and I opened my eyes.

There was the sound again! I ran back to the tracks and in the distance, saw a tiny plume of black smoke. I held my breath and clenched my hands under my chin. Slowly, the round face of a locomotive appeared. As it chugged closer, the face grew larger and the wailing grew louder. My heart pounded as it approached the station. The bell clanged and steam hissed from under the engine before it finally came to a stop.

The only passenger to get off was a girl about my age. She had long blonde hair and wore a flowered cotton dress. With help from the conductor, she tugged a large, brown leather suitcase onto the platform. She caught my eye and walked toward me. As she got closer, her perfect complexion and bright blue eyes prompted me to run my hand through my own short, dark hair.

"Hi! I'm Mabel Anderson." The girl held out her hand and smiled.

I shook her hand vigorously. "I'm so glad to see someone else!" I pointed to my trunk. "I'm trying to get to Purdue. I thought there would be taxis here."

"They'll show up later in the day when more students arrive."

"How do you know that?"

"My uncle works at Purdue. We can take the trolley, but we have to carry our luggage to the 'Purdue Only' stop on Main Street. By the way, what's your name?"

"Oh, sorry! I'm Ginny Ross." I stuck out my hand and we shook again.

We decided the best way to move our luggage was to carry both pieces together, so we dragged Mabel's suitcase on top of the trunk. We grasped the trunk's handles at either end and lifted. A strip of dry grass at the side of the station led to a street lined with more red brick buildings.

"This is Second Street," Mabel said. "We'll follow it to Main Street and pick up the trolley there."

"Where is everybody?" I asked. The street was strangely silent—no vehicles, no voices, and no sounds from the open windows of the apartments above the stores.

"It's Sunday morning," Mabel explained. "The stores and factories in this part of town are all closed. People are in church or in bed."

We didn't walk very far before we had to stop for a rest. We stretched our backs and shook out our arms.

"Is it always this hot?" I asked, fanning myself with my hand.

"The newspaper says we're setting heat records this summer."

The sweat running down my back prompted me to nod in agreement.

I dried my hands on my skirt before we lifted again. The process was slow but talking helped to pass the time. I found out that Mabel lived on a farm and had two brothers who were studying at Purdue, as well as the uncle who worked there. I told her that I lived with my Mom, brother Billy, and Nana. My papa died four years ago but we still lived above the store he used to run. My dad was in Toronto looking for work but he wasn't having much luck.

Mabel smiled at me. "I can tell by your accent that you're not from around here."

"I'm from Newfoundland," I said proudly. "It's a six-day journey by train and ferry."

"Wow! You must be exhausted."

"That," I said with a sigh, "is for sure."

We managed to cover a whole block before we stopped to rest in the entrance to one of the closed stores. The awning created enough shade to lower the temperature by a few degrees. We sat side by side on the front step.

"So, what course are you taking?" I asked her.

"Home economics. And you?"

"Mechanical engineering."

Mabel frowned. "Mechanical engineering?"

"Yes, what's wrong with that?"

"But...." Mabel seemed genuinely confused. "Everyone knows engineering is for men."

I turned to look at her. "Don't let Amelia Earhart hear you say that. She thinks women can do anything men can do—and so do I."

"But what's so special about mechanical engineering?"

"If I'm going to be a pilot, I have to know all about engines."

"*You're* going to be a pilot?" She stared at me with her eyes wide.

"Just like Amelia."

Mabel scrutinized me, trying to figure out if I was pulling her leg. "And fly across the Atlantic Ocean?"

I nodded. "That's the plan."

"Right!" She stood up and smoothed the front of her dress. "Time to move this load before you completely lose your mind."

We picked up the trunk and continued walking. "On our farm, everyone has a specific job," Mabel said. "My dad doesn't bake the bread and my mom doesn't plow the fields."

Before I could reply, the trolley came into view.

"Oh, no! We're not at the stop yet." I looked at Mabel, who calmly told me not to worry. With her arm in the air, she walked to the middle of Main Street. The trolley slowed and stopped. The driver hopped out and helped us carry our luggage on board.

"My money is in my trunk," I whispered to Mabel.

"Don't worry. I'll pay for both of us and you can pay me back later." She dropped the coins into the box and we sat down.

I took a deep breath and let it out slowly. For the first time in six days, I felt my shoulders relaxing. I was almost there—and I wasn't alone anymore.

CHAPTER 2

PURDUE UNIVERSITY

———◅◦▻———

I GAZED THROUGH the trolley window at the stores on Main Street—J. C. Penney, Hurley and Sons Grocery, and H. M. Bahl's Hardware. When we came to a bridge, Mabel told me we were crossing the Wabash River into West Lafayette.

On the other side, the landscape changed from fields, to houses, and then, at the top of a steep hill, into more shops. Five minutes later, large, red brick buildings appeared in a grassy area, surrounded by a few trees.

My heart raced. "Is this it?"

Before Mabel could answer the driver announced, "Purdue University, ladies!"

We thanked him and slid our luggage down the trolley's steps.

"The Women's Residence is still a few blocks from here," Mabel said as she dragged her suitcase over to my trunk. "We'd better keep moving."

We lifted our load and started walking again. The sun continued to beat down on us so we headed for the shade at the side of the road. After a few minutes, Mabel spoke again.

"By the way, how do you know what Amelia Earhart thinks and says?"

"I've met her."

Mabel's end of the trunk crashed to the ground. "You've met Amelia Earhart? *The* Amelia Earhart?"

"Twice," I replied as I lowered my end of the trunk.

"Where? When? How?"

I held up my hands as if I was surrendering. Mabel laughed, turned her suitcase sideways on the trunk, and sat down. She held out her hand for me to continue.

"Where should I start?"

"At the beginning, of course!"

I sat down and folded my hands on my lap. "The first time I met Amelia I was twelve years old. I ran away from home to find her because I figured she could help me arrange flying lessons."

"Did you find her?"

"Yes, at her house in Rye, New York. She said I had to finish school first, but then she'd do what she could." I took something out of my pocket and handed it to Mabel. "Amelia gave me this silver four-leaf clover for luck, and some money to get back home to Harbour Grace."

"Wow!" Mabel took the clover and rubbed it between her fingers. "So, where did you meet her the second time?"

"At Aunt Rose's hotel a few months later—May 20, 1932, to be exact. Amelia was in Harbour Grace to rest and refuel after her flight from the mainland. Later that day she planned to take off on her solo transatlantic flight." I glanced at Mabel and grinned. "And I helped her."

Mabel scoffed. "How could *you* help Amelia Earhart?"

"When she landed, I noticed one of the wheels on her plane jumped each time it rotated. I told my uncle Harry, who is the airstrip supervisor. He and Amelia's team checked it out and they found a piece of metal lodged in the tire. She said I prevented a blowout and possibly a crash."

"Really?"

"She also said she thought I'd make a good pilot." I spread my hands out and looked around at the Purdue buildings. "So here I am."

"What does she look like in real life? Is she pretty?"

"Very pretty." I knew from Mabel's expression that she was eager to hear a lot more about Amelia. "But maybe we should keep walking while we talk."

Mabel gazed at the clover and then passed it back. We stood up and lifted the trunk again.

"Do you know why Amelia always smiles with her mouth closed?" I asked.

"No, why?"

"She has a big space between her front teeth. She said you could drive a truck through it."

Mabel glanced at me. "Is it that wide?"

"No. Amelia was just trying to tell me that she's not as pretty as everyone thinks. In most of her pictures her hair has been curled and she's wearing makeup."

"Really?"

"That's what she told me."

Talking about Amelia made the walk seem shorter and the load lighter. But I fell silent when the Women's Residence came into view. Tall oaks stood in front of a huge red brick building. White stone surrounded big bay windows on the second and third floors.

I slowly lowered my end of the trunk and stared. It wasn't just the impressive size; it was what the building represented. This would be my home for the next four years—four years away from everything and everyone I knew and loved.

"Are you all right?" Mabel lowered her end of the trunk and stood next to me.

"Just taking in my new home."

I swallowed the growing lump in my throat. It was time to let go of Harbour Grace. My head knew this was true but my heart wasn't there yet. I found myself blinking back tears for the second time that day.

Mabel looked at me with concern. I smiled to show her I was fine and we lifted the trunk together.

"Let's get a closer look," I said.

We walked up the driveway and found the same white stone framed the front door. I held it open and Mabel pushed the trunk and suitcase inside. One more flight of stairs and we stood in the foyer.

"Whew!" I wiped my forehead with the back of my hand. "I'm sweating something awful."

"I think you mean perspiring." Mabel dabbed her face with a lace-trimmed hanky.

"Sorry. I'm *perspiring* something awful." I tried to pull my skirt off my sticky legs but soon gave up. The foyer had grabbed my attention. It looked like nothing I'd ever seen before. The ceiling soared above my head. The space was twice the size of the living room and dining room put together back home. I bent down and ran my fingers along the floor. "The tiles look like river stones in a shallow stream," I told Mabel.

"Get up," she whispered.

I jumped up and straightened my skirt, just as a woman with short brown hair entered the foyer. She smiled and walked toward us.

"Welcome ladies. I'm Miss Schleman, director of the Women's Residence." She shook hands with Mabel, who introduced herself, and I did the same. "You're the first to arrive. Would you like to room together?"

Mabel looked at me and smiled. "Welcome to Purdue, roomie!"

I grabbed her hands and squeezed them. "Thanks, roomie!"

Miss Schleman laughed. "I couldn't have said it better myself, Mabel." She handed us an envelope with our room number on it. "Your keys are inside."

Our room on the second floor had two single beds on either side of the door, a dresser and closet for each of us against the side walls, and two desks and chairs under the windows at the far end.

Mabel twirled around. "I can't believe all this is ours!"

We inspected the closets, the view from our windows, and the softness of the beds. The common bathroom at the end of the hall had three separate cubicles, with a bathtub and a wooden chair in each. Mabel thought a bath would do us a world of good and I agreed.

We got soap and towels from our room and were soon up to our necks in cool water. It wasn't as cold as the salt water in the bay back home, but it felt some nice all the same.

Back in our room, we changed into clean clothes and opened the windows. With our elbows on the sills, we leaned out. The oak leaves threw dappled sunlight onto the grass and bird songs filled the still air. Any remaining tension from the last six days left my body. The long train and ferry rides were over, I had a new friend, and I was where I should be, when I said I would be there. I tried to stifle a yawn but it was no use. I walked to my bed and stretched out.

Mabel hesitated by the window. "Will you do me a favour?"

"Sure."

"Will you introduce me to Amelia Earhart?"

"Of course." It was the least I could do after she'd rescued me at the train station.

"Thanks!" Mabel walked to her own bed and sat down.

She continued chatting but my mind had floated back to Harbour Grace. I heard the Salvation Army Band playing the "Ode to Newfoundland" outside Papa's store on the day I left for Purdue. The whole town had come out to see me off.

Llewellyn and Uncle Harry carried my trunk and a procession of family and friends followed us down Water Street. People leaned out of windows and doorways. "Good luck, Ginny!" they shouted. "Show dem b'ys what you're about."

At the station, the conductor showed Llewellyn and Uncle Harry where to put my trunk and I boarded the train. From the window, I saw Mom wiping her eyes while Uncle Harry patted her back. Aunt Rose held Nana's arm and Llewellyn stood with his arm draped around my brother Billy's shoulders.

The train lurched forward and everyone waved and cheered. Llewellyn shouted something I couldn't hear so I pushed down the window. He ran beside the train and shouted, "Don't forget, Gin. You're our Amelia Earhart." As the train pulled away from him, he gave me a thumbs-up. I waved back.

Thinking of Llewellyn made me smile, but also made my heart ache.

"You're our Amelia Earhart," I repeated to myself before I fell asleep.

CHAPTER 3

AIRPORT

———◄○►———

I WOKE TO the sound of voices in the hallway and looked over at Mabel. She was lying on her bed, reading. The clock on her bedside table told me it was almost dinnertime.

"I just heard one of them is taking mechanical engineering," a voice from the hallway said. "Wait 'til she meets Professor Jones." Soft laughter faded down the hall.

I sat up and swung my legs over the side of the bed. "Who's this Professor Jones?"

"He's my uncle." Mabel closed the book and set it on her bedside table. "The one who works here. You'll like him."

"I'm sure I will." I smiled at my new friend but couldn't help wondering why her uncle's name sounded so ominous.

Before our conversation could continue, the dinner bell rang. Mabel and I headed downstairs and fell in with a noisy crowd moving toward the dining room. None of the other girls were as beautiful as Mabel but they were all just as well dressed. They wore lipstick and smelled good too, like fancy soap or perfume. I felt like an imposter among the smart, floral dresses and shining hair. I was tempted to give my armpits a sniff, just to make sure I wasn't "perspiring" again.

We inched forward until I saw Miss Schleman standing next to a large fireplace at the far end of the dining room. Light coloured oak tables and chairs stood in front of her. Portraits of middle-aged women covered the wall to my right and on the opposite wall tall windows filled the room with late afternoon light. We filed in, looked for our name tags, and sat down.

Breathe, I told myself. *You're doing fine.* With my hands tightly clasped in my lap, I looked around the table.

"Hi, I'm Elizabeth from South Bend," the girl next to Mabel said.

"Pleased to meet you. I'm Mabel from Milroy."

"Hi, Mabel. This is my roommate, Sarah, from Dayton, Ohio."

"Hi, Sarah," Mabel replied. "This is my roommate, Ginny, from Harbour Grace, Newfoundland."

"Newfoundland?" The word went around the table until Elizabeth asked the question. "Where exactly is that?"

"It's an island off the east coast of Canada," I told them.

"What's Harbour Grace like?" a girl farther down the table asked.

I took a deep breath and described the first things that came to my mind when I thought of home: the smell of the salt air, the feel of a cool wind off the bay on a hot day, and the sound of the gulls screeching at the town wharf when the fishing boats unloaded their catch. I unclasped my hands to demonstrate how to jig for cod and as I talked, my heart rate slowly returned to normal.

"Tell them how long it took you to get here," Mabel prompted me.

"Two days on the train to get to Port aux Basques. That's on the opposite coast from Harbour Grace," I explained. "Then one day on the ferry to get to Nova Scotia. And then three more days on different trains to get to Boston, New York, Chicago, and finally to West Lafayette."

"And I thought travelling from Indianapolis was a big deal!" Sarah exclaimed.

The girls discussed my trip amongst themselves and the introductions continued. By the time the roast beef dinner arrived, we realized we were all in the same hallway on the second floor.

As tea and dessert were served, Miss Schleman stood up and formally welcomed us. She said we could get back to socializing after she made a few announcements: "More students will arrive tomorrow afternoon. If you could please pick up your class schedules and textbooks in the morning, it will reduce the strain on my office and the bookstore. As well as meals, afternoon tea will be served in this dining room each day at three o'clock until classes begin."

"I need a compass set as well," I whispered to Mabel.

"Don't worry. You can get it at the bookstore when we get our books."

Back upstairs the girls in our hallway went from room to room admiring the clothes the others had brought. I sat on my bed and greeted them but I couldn't understand half of what they said about hems and collars. To me a dress was green or blue, short or long. I'd never heard of "cut on the bias" or "hand smocked." Instead of saying the wrong thing and looking silly, I stayed quiet.

Once our room was empty, I stood up and walked to the window. I pulled back the drapes and looked out. Starlight sparkled like fairy dust across the navy sky. I imagined Llewellyn looking at the same sky. He would be standing at the railing of his ship, somewhere off the coast of Newfoundland.

From the first moment I told him I wanted to be a pilot, he'd encouraged me. "If anyone can do it, it's you, Gin!" I saw his smiling face and the freckles across his nose. A fluttering in my chest reminded me of how much I missed his hands on either side of my face and his lips gently kissing my forehead.

I turned around to find Mabel hemming a skirt. "Do you want to go to the afternoon tea tomorrow?"

Mabel's hand stopped moving and she looked up. "Not especially. What do you have in mind?"

I smiled. "Will you take me to the airport?"

⟨○⟩

By ten o'clock the next morning, we had purchased our books and supplies and picked up our class schedules. We dropped everything off in our room and were on our way. It was still cool and the walk to the airport was pleasant. Trees lined the road, behind which rolled endless cornfields. After fifteen minutes, we saw the top of the control tower. I picked up the pace and soon we were looking at big white letters, PURDUE UNIVERSITY AIRPORT. Through the open doors of the huge hangar, we saw two planes.

I walked to the closest one and ran my hands over the fuselage. "This is my third experience with a Lockheed Vega," I told Mabel in a hushed voice. "My first was the City of New York when it landed at the airstrip in Harbour Grace. It was painted maroon, with cream-coloured wings and its name in cream letters down the sides. When the watchman wasn't looking, I snuck inside and pretended I was flying."

When Mabel didn't reply, I turned around and found her standing with her mouth open and her arms hanging at her sides. I waved her over and she stood beside me, looking up at the plane.

"My second experience was with the red Vega that Amelia flew from Harbour Grace to Ireland. She called it her 'little red bus' because it had no name. Her publicist wanted people to remember her name, not the name of the plane."

Mabel still stood silently beside me. She looked the way I felt when the girls had been talking about fashion. I wanted to put her at ease.

"You can touch it," I encouraged her. "You won't hurt it."

She stepped forward and tentatively placed her hand next to mine.

"This plane has the same maroon and beige colour as the City of New York but, see, they replaced the name with Purdue University." I walked toward the back of the plane, still running my hands along the fuselage. "Feel how smooth the wooden siding is."

Mabel followed me and nodded. But instead of running her hand along the siding, like me, she stroked the plane as if she was petting a horse on her family's farm.

"Hey!"

We both jumped. A boy with short blond hair stood on the other side of the hangar, wiping his hands on a cloth. He walked toward us with long, confident strides, as if to show us this was his place and we didn't belong there.

Mabel froze but I walked forward to meet him. "Lockheed Vegas are my favourite planes."

His eyes narrowed. "And how do you know it's a Vega?"

"My Uncle Harry has been teaching me about planes for years."

We faced each other in the middle of the hangar. I looked up into the bluest eyes I'd ever seen—but they weren't exactly friendly.

"Let's see what Uncle Harry taught you about engines," he challenged. "I can't get this one to start."

He turned and walked back to where we'd first seen him.

Mabel was still standing frozen next to the plane so I waved her over. Together we followed the blond boy to a workbench on the opposite side of the hangar.

I looked at the engine in front of us. "Wait, isn't this from a car?"

"We start with small engines and work our way up to locomotives and planes," the boy replied.

I put my hands on the engine and poked here and there. "It doesn't seem to be the electrical connections but there's a strong smell of gasoline. Maybe it's the float. Over time the dope coating can develop cracks and the cork starts to absorb fuel and become heavy."

"Can you fix it?"

"If you get me a new float, I'll give it a try."

The boy left while I disassembled the carburetor.

"Ginny!" Mabel whispered. "Do you really think you should be doing that?"

"Trust me," I whispered back. "I've done this before."

When he returned with the float, I used it to replace the old one. I put the carburetor back in the engine and set the carburetor controls. "Let's fire it up and see if it works."

The engine coughed a few times and then began to roar. Mabel covered her ears and the boy's eyes opened wide. "Uncle Harry must be a great teacher!" he shouted over the noise.

I smiled and nodded before turning off the engine.

"I'm Matt Baker." He held out his hand and when he smiled, his eyes crinkled in the corners. The blue looked a little warmer now.

"I'm Ginny Ross and this is my roommate, Mabel Anderson." I held out my hand.

Mabel burst out laughing at the sight of my hand. "What a mess!"

Matt picked up a towel from under the workbench and I wiped off as much of the grease as I could. We all shook hands and then Matt restarted the engine. The hangar filled with noise and an older man walked in.

Matt turned off the engine as the man approached the workbench.

"Nice work," the man said to Matt.

"Ginny fixed it," Matt said.

"Really?" The man looked at me.

Matt told him about Uncle Harry's lessons but the older man still looked impressed. He asked me a few questions and nodded as I answered. He extended his hand first to me, and then Mabel. "I'm Captain Aretz, the airport manager. But you can just call me Cap. Why don't you come back tomorrow and show me what else you know about engines?"

"Sure!" I replied. "May I bring Mabel with me?"

"Yes, of course," Cap turned and told Mabel she was welcome any time.

I excused myself to wash my hands properly. In the small bathroom, I turned on the tap and looked in the mirror over the sink. A smile stretched from one side of my face to the other. "You're supposed to be a serious, rational, would-be pilot," I whispered to my reflection. But the goofy grin remained.

When I turned off the tap, I heard voices outside the door. I quickly dried my hands and stepped back into the hangar.

Mabel stood there frowning as Cap and Matt disappeared into another room.

"Mabel, is something wrong?" I asked.

She looked at me. "Matt said you sure know a lot about planes but he wonders what Professor Jones will think of that."

Professor Jones again. First the girls outside our door at the residence and now Matt. There was something about the way people said this man's name that caused butterflies in my stomach.

"Why would Matt say that?" Mabel asked me.

I couldn't answer because I was asking myself the same question.

CHAPTER 4

REGISTRATION

————◆◇◆————

THE SHRILL CRY of a blue jay woke me the next morning. I opened my eyes to sunshine spilling into the room from a crack between the drapes. I turned my head to find Mabel's bed was empty. *What did you expect?* I asked myself. *Your roomie is a farm girl who has probably been up for hours.*

I sat up. Cap Aretz had invited us back to the airport! But before I could fully enjoy that thought, Professor Jones's grey, unformed figure popped into my mind—something like the Ghost of Christmas Yet to Come.

I flopped back on the bed and put my hands on my head. "Okay," I said out loud. "Make a decision. You can be dragged down by Professor Jones before you even meet him or you can have fun here." I kicked the sheets to the end of the bed and stood up. I was going to have fun here!

Just as I started making my bed, Mabel walked in the door. "Good morning, sleepyhead," she said. At her dresser, she dropped her toothbrush into a glass and picked up a tube of lipstick. She lightly dabbed her lips and pressed them together. Then she dabbed some on her cheeks and rubbed it in. I pretended to smooth my bedspread but I was really watching every move she made.

Mabel held out the lipstick. "You can borrow some if you like."

"Thanks, but I've...never worn it before."

"You're eighteen years old and you've *never* worn lipstick?"

I paused. I'd been dreading any discussion about my age. "Actually...I'm sixteen."

"How can you be in university if you're only sixteen?"

"In Newfoundland, we finish high school after grade eleven," I explained. "It's the British system."

"Really?"

I nodded and looked Mabel in the eyes. "But listen, I'd prefer if you didn't tell anyone. I already feel like a fish out of water."

Mabel laughed. "I presume that's a Newfoundland expression, but I get the picture. Your secret is safe with me." She took one last look in the mirror and dropped the lipstick tube in her pocket.

"Are you coming to the airport with me?" I asked as I struggled to pull a dress over my head.

"Just as soon as we register."

"Didn't we do that yesterday?"

Mabel explained we'd picked up our course schedules and textbooks. Now we had to confirm our courses with the registrar, to show him we didn't want to make any changes. We also had to choose the clubs we wanted to join.

"I'm not much of a joiner," I said. "And I can't think of any club that would want me. I can't sing, dance, act, play a musical instrument, hit a ball...."

"How about an engineering club?"

I perked up. I hadn't thought of that. "That might work!"

We hurried downstairs and out the front door. Mabel said if we got to the Armory early, the line-ups wouldn't be too long. As we walked down State Street, I wondered what I would have done without her. When I arrived, I didn't know anything about West Lafayette, the trolley, the Women's Residence, or Purdue. I reached out and touched her elbow.

"Thanks for taking such good care of me."

"Hey, I live here," she said with a good–natured shrug. "You'd do the same for me in Harbour Grace."

"You bet I would!" I slipped my arm around Mabel's elbow and we continued walking.

At University Street we turned left and suddenly people seemed to come from every direction. Mabel explained that the Armory was just up ahead.

It was yet another two-storey red brick building, but this one was attached to a larger structure with a round roof. *There must be a factory nearby*, I thought. It seemed the only way to explain all this brick. Mabel and I surged through the big double doors with the rest of the crowd and waved to the girls from our residence.

The post office back home was big, but nothing like this. The ceiling rose three storeys above the floor and was supported by huge metal beams. Sunshine flooded in through big windows at the front and back.

Tables and chairs stood around the perimeter, with more in the middle of the open space. People sat behind the tables with colourful papers spread out in front of them. Banners with strange names hung from the walls—Omnicron Nu, Pi Tau Sigma, and Tau Beta Pi.

"Why are all those people just sitting there?" I asked.

"They represent the clubs we can join," she explained. "But we have to see the registrar first."

Mabel grabbed my hand and we pushed through the throng of students. Ten people stood ahead of us in the registrar's line. "When we get to the table," she said, "just follow my lead."

While we waited, she named the clubs she wanted to join—the band because she played clarinet, and Omnicron Nu because it was a national home economics society. "They're very welcoming and helpful to freshmen," she told me.

I nodded and looked around the room.

"Don't worry," she said, watching me take everything in. "We'll find some engineering clubs for you."

It was Mabel's turn with the registrar. "Mabel Anderson," she said as she placed her class schedule in front of a man wearing wire-rimmed glasses. He asked if she wanted to make any changes and she said no thank you. He stamped her paper and passed it to a young woman sitting beside him. She found a place for it in the box marked *Freshman Home Economics*. Mabel stepped away.

I placed my paper on the table. "Ginny Ross," I said.

The man in the glasses looked at my schedule and then back at me. "Any changes?" he asked.

"No, thank you."

"Are you sure?" he peered at me over the top of his glasses.

"I'm sure." I looked him in the eyes and hoped he saw the determination in mine.

"Well, you have a month to make up your mind," he said with a shrug. "After that you're stuck with your choice."

My heart pounded. I knew I could learn to fly a plane but could I learn to deal with people who didn't believe in me? *This is no time to lose your confidence*, I told myself. I stood up a little straighter, looked the registrar in the eyes, and replied, "Thank you for the information."

He stamped my sheet and the young woman filed it in the box marked *Freshman Mechanical Engineering*. When I backed away from the table, I caught him whispering something to the young woman who smiled and nodded.

"Looks like I'm not the only one who thinks you're crazy," Mabel whispered.

"Then why are you so interested in Amelia Earhart?"

"She's the exception."

"So am I."

Mabel shook her head and patted my arm, as if I were some deluded person who needed sympathy. Then she led me around the Armory until she found the clubs she wanted to join.

"If we go to the tables where boys are lined up," she said, "we'll probably find engineering clubs for you."

That proved to be a good idea. At the banner marked Pi Tau Sigma, Mabel picked up a brochure and read the conditions for membership. "Members are chosen on the basis of engineering ability, scholarship, and personality," she read aloud.

"I'll never get into that club," I whispered. "They'll reject me because of my personality."

"But they don't even know you."

"They don't have to know me," I replied. "They'll just reject me because I'm a girl and then claim it was because of my personality."

"Why would you let people treat you like that?" Mabel asked.

"Amelia says when a woman tries to do a man's job, people react negatively. She calls being a pilot a 'non-traditional role' for a woman."

Mabel put the brochure down. "Then I guess we'd better find you a non-traditional club."

It wasn't exactly a vote of confidence, but at least she was no longer suggesting I'd lost my mind.

We stopped at many tables before we found a club that sounded promising.

"Tau Beta Pi," I read aloud, "is an engineering society that bases membership on scholarship, the spirit of liberal culture, and distinction in the field of engineering."

"You may as well test their definition of 'liberal culture,'" Mabel said, and passed me an application form.

I signed and handed it to one of the boys behind the table. He read it, smirked, and handed it to the boy next to him.

"Wait 'til Professor Jones sees this," the boy whispered before he dropped my application into the box.

We moved away from the table and Mabel held out her hands. "Why do people keep saying my uncle's name like that?"

"Maybe he thinks women shouldn't get an education."

"It's definitely not that," Mabel said. "He's paying my tuition—my brothers' too. If it wasn't for him, my family couldn't afford university."

I turned to Mabel and looked her in the eyes. "I've decided not to let anyone spoil my time here. Maybe you should do the same."

"I will!" Mabel took my hand and together we walked out of the Armory.

CHAPTER 5

TAYLOR CUB

——◀◉▶——

B ACK IN THE warmth of the early fall day, Mabel and I walked in the direction of the university airport. Blue jays called to each other. Men's voices floated out of the cornfields along the road. Mabel explained that the fall harvest had begun.

Never in my wildest dreams had I imagined a place like Indiana. I wished Llewellyn could see me—a university student walking to the Purdue Airport because the manager wanted to see what else she knew about planes. I imagined Llew smiling, touching my cheek, and telling me how proud he was of everything I was accomplishing.

The control tower appeared on the horizon and drew us like a magnet. Our leisurely pace became a steady run that ended in front of the hangar. Mabel and I bent over to catch our breath before we entered.

The Lockheed Vega was still there. I laid my hands and forehead on its fuselage. There were so many reasons I longed to be a pilot—adventure, freedom, money for my family, and work I loved. My goal felt so much closer when I was actually touching a plane. Mabel joined me and put her hands on it too.

I turned to her and whispered, "This is where I belong."

"I hope you're right," Mabel whispered back.

Cap Aretz shouted, "Hi girls," across the hangar.

I patted the plane once more and then followed Mabel across the huge space.

"Are you ready to show me what you know about engines, Ginny?" Cap asked.

"Ready when you are," I said. After the tension of registration and the club selection, it was a relief to talk to someone who was willing to give me a chance.

We walked to a small red-and-white plane on the opposite side of the hangar. I looked over the fuselage at Cap. "This is the tiniest plane I've ever seen!"

"It's a Taylor Cub," he told me. "We use it for training student pilots. Show me how you would service it and explain what you're doing out loud."

I considered the plane, and decided to start with the obvious. "Are there any known problems with this one?"

"No," Cap replied. "This is just a routine servicing after thirty hours of operation."

I took a deep breath and put my hands on the engine. "Okay, my friend, let's see how you look inside." I looked up at Cap and said, "Will you help me remove the cowlings?"

"The what?" Mabel interjected.

"The engine covers," Cap explained.

Mabel blushed. "Sorry." She made a zipping motion over her mouth.

"Don't ever be sorry for asking questions!" he told her. "It's the only way to learn." He waved Mabel over and the three of us laid the cowlings on the floor.

I started to walk around the plane but Cap stopped me before I got all the way around. I'd forgotten to describe what I was doing out loud. I cleared my throat before I spoke.

"I'll make a general examination for external damage." I walked around the plane, touched a few spots, and looked underneath. "Now I'll check for oil, fuel, or exhaust leaks. Do you have a flashlight I can use?"

Cap pulled one out of his jacket pocket and handed it to me. I looked around and behind the engine for several minutes.

"Everything looks clean so I'll check the magneto timing." I pointed to a cylinder, set on its side at the back of the engine, and looked up at Mabel. "The magneto creates an electrical current, which is sent to the spark plug. Then the spark plug ignites the fuel. I have to make sure the timing is set right for the process to work."

"Kind of like a chain reaction?" Mabel asked.

I gave her a thumbs-up and then shone the flashlight behind the engine. "Fine so far," I said. "The next job is to clean and gap the spark plugs and replace any that need it."

Just as I turned back to the engine I saw Matt, the tall blond boy from the day before. He didn't say a word to anyone, just peeked over Mabel's shoulder. When I looked up again, he was rubbing his greasy hands on a towel.

I smiled at him and turned to Cap. "I've just about completed the inspection."

"Good. What's next?"

"I'll check the air and gas filters and the oil filter cartridge."

"Tell me what you need," Matt said. "I'll get it for you."

I leaned over the engine again and poked around. "I may as well change all three of them." Matt walked to a cupboard on the opposite wall, found what he wanted, and returned to the plane. He took the old filters from me and handed me the new ones as I needed them.

"Now I'll check the carburetor to make sure the float is functioning properly."

"Good," Cap said. "That's a problem the boys sometimes miss."

I smiled at Matt and saw him blush. "I'll probably need a new float," I told him.

When the servicing was finished, I wiped my greasy hands on the towel Matt handed me. It was time to perform a ground run to see if my servicing was successful. The four of us pushed the plane out onto the runway and Cap asked me to start it up.

I could hardly believe my ears. I hesitated. "Really?"

"You serviced it," Cap replied. "You start it."

I stepped into the Taylor Cub's tiny cockpit and rubbed my hands together. The switches and dials on the instrument panel looked just like the ones in the City of New York. I took a deep breath and rested my hand on the throttle. Outside, Matt turned the propeller and a roar echoed in the autumn air. He cheered, Mabel's eyes widened, Cap smiled, and I heaved a huge sigh of relief.

When I turned off the engine, Matt said, "She knows more about planes than any girl I've ever met!"

"She's one of a kind all right," Cap replied with a smile.

I stepped out of the plane and curtsied. Mabel just shook her head in amazement.

"You deserve a break after all that work. Let's take a spin around the campus," Cap said, patting the plane and looking at me.

My heart skipped a beat. "You're kidding!"

"I never kid when it comes to planes," Cap replied. "This one needs a flight check before the boys start their aviation classes."

He held his hand out to me. I stepped over the low door again and sat in the back seat. Cap stepped into the front seat, pulled the door up and the window down. I clasped my hands in my lap and breathed in the smell of leather seats and machine oil. This was it. I was finally going into the air!

Cap signalled Matt to turn the propeller. I took a deep breath as another roar filled the air. The wheels turned slowly and the plane rolled to the runway closest to the hangar. My heart pounded as Cap revved the engine to full power, eased the throttle forward, and started our takeoff run. The runway blurred with the increased speed and the force pushed me back in my seat. My stomach gave a lurch as the ground fell away, and my whole body tingled with the vibration. Mabel, Matt, and the hangar got smaller and smaller as we soared into the clear blue sky.

All my studying with Uncle Harry had taught me what to expect during takeoff. But knowing was not the same as feeling. I wanted to hold my hands over my head and yell, "I'm free!" No more a fish out of water. I was an eagle, soaring, gliding, and swooping through the clouds. This was where an eagle belonged.

The roaring of the wind and the engine made talking difficult. Cap turned his head and yelled something to me that sounded like "football." I looked down where he was pointing and saw a huge green oval with white lines. Mabel had told me the football stadium was at the end of University Street, so now I had a landmark. I recognized the Armory, with its sloping roof and big windows. When Cap flew over, the students streaming in and out looked up and waved.

We continued south, where the buildings stood closer together. I wasn't sure what I was looking at, but was impressed with how much bigger the university looked from the air. Obviously, I'd only seen a small part of it from the ground.

I gazed beyond the buildings to clumps of dark green trees and open yellow fields. The corn stalks seemed to bow their heads as Cap and I flew over. In the pastures, cows grazed and horses ran away from the roar of the plane.

Cap turned around again and shouted over his shoulder. I heard "Time...home." I smiled and nodded, although I hated to leave the sky.

Cap flew over more buildings until I recognized the airport runways in the distance. Slowly we lost altitude and the buildings, cars, and people grew. We bounced down onto solid ground and taxied back to the hangar, where Mabel and Matt still stood on the tarmac. They ran toward the plane as soon as it stopped. Cap pushed the window up and the door down. Then Matt held out his hand and I stepped out.

"What was it like?" Mabel asked right away.

"Amazing!" I practically shouted.

Cap stepped out of the plane and I turned to him. "Thank you so much!" I took his hand in both of mine and shook it vigorously.

He chuckled. "Keep up the good work and you'll be flying the plane yourself in no time."

"That's my plan!"

"Amelia Earhart will be on campus soon," Cap said. "I know she wants to talk to people like you about aviation."

"She already—" Mabel started, but a frown from me made her stop. "That's a good idea," she said instead.

"A *very* good idea," I agreed. I held out my hand to Cap again. "Thank you. This was the best present anyone has ever given me."

He laughed and said I was more than welcome. Mabel and I said goodbye and walked in the direction of our residence.

My whole body still tingled from the flight. I'd often thought of what it would be like to fly, but to feel it was more thrilling than I'd imagined—the smell of machine oil and leather, the roar of the engine, and the whole world stretching out below. More than all of that was the sense of freedom. I couldn't stop smiling.

"You could have knocked me over with a feather when you stepped out of that plane!" Mabel's voice brought me back to earth.

"Still think I'm crazy?"

She shook her head, but there was a sparkle in her eye this time. "Only slightly."

"Gee, thanks."

We both laughed and continued walking, until Mabel stopped again.

"Why didn't you want me to tell Cap you already know Amelia?"

I headed to the side of the road and sat down on the grass. "It's this whole 'non-traditional role' idea. Being in engineering already has people talking about me. I don't want to draw more attention to myself."

Mabel sat down beside me. "Wait 'til they find out you want to be a pilot!"

"I'm not looking forward to that reaction." I thought for a few more seconds. "I'm different enough for now. Telling people I know Amelia can wait until she arrives."

"Should we keep your flight with Cap a secret too?"

"Definitely! It could ruin my chance of being elected homecoming queen."

Mabel burst out laughing. "I think your chance disappeared a long time ago!"

She stood up and adjusted an imaginary crown. Strutting back and forth with her nose in the air, she waved regally to her subjects. When her feet got tangled in the tall grass and she fell over, our laughter echoed across the cornfields.

CHAPTER 6

PROFESSOR JONES

————◀○▶————

THE NEXT MORNING, the dining room was full. This was the first day of classes.

"You've got the right room but the wrong building," Mabel was telling Faye.

A class schedule passed under my nose. Even though I wasn't part of the conversation, I passed cereal, juice, and milk whenever people asked for them. I already knew my first class was with Professor Jones, and no one from the residence would be there. At least I'd finally find out what he was really like.

After we finished eating, we walked as a group to the Home Economics Building. All the girls headed in except Mabel. "I'll show Ginny how to find her building," she told the others. "Then I'll be back."

Mabel kept to the main streets instead of cutting across campus. "Once you know your way around, I'll show you the shortcuts."

We walked a bit farther down State Street and then turned left at Marstellar Street. At the traffic circle, we turned right. Mechanical engineering was the second building on the right.

Mabel stopped and looked into my eyes. "In spite of what you've been hearing, Uncle Malcolm is a kind man." She gave me a quick hug. "You'll see how much his students like him."

"I'm sure I will. Thanks for walking me here." I smiled at Mabel and moved toward the front steps. She headed back the way we came.

Male students turned to look at me but no one said a word. They nudged each other and snickered instead. I kept my eyes down and walked through the front door. I had planned to walk up the stairs with my head held high. I would give a haughty glance to any male students who reacted to me in a negative way. But in reality, my stomach churned and a sense of fear kept my eyes on my feet.

My shoulders relaxed when the heavy main door banged shut behind me. I took a few deep breaths and walked slowly along the inside hall. A high ceiling made my footsteps echo and the terrazzo floor smelled of fresh wax.

The doors into the classrooms were numbered. I looked for 132. Because the first number was a one, I thought it might be on the ground floor. And there it was, on the left just before a long flight of stairs leading to the second floor.

I opened the door to a large, empty classroom and sat at the front table. A type of counter faced me, with a small engine at one end. It looked like it came from a car. The door opened and a small group of boys walked in. They stopped momentarily when they saw me, looked at each other, and continued to seats somewhere in the back. I heard them whispering as they sat down.

I couldn't remember smiling at them so I decided to try this when the door opened again. A lone boy walked in, looked at my smiling face, smiled back, and found a seat behind me. *Hey*, I thought, *this is working*. Next, a large group entered, laughing, shoving each other, and banging into the desks and chairs. I smiled but none of them looked my way.

A few minutes passed before the door crashed open and I recognized some of the boys from the front steps. They crowded around me and leaned into my face. I tried to pull away but they'd circled behind.

"And what do we have here?" one of them said.

"I do believe it's a female of the species," a second replied. My head swivelled from one boy to the other.

Two more started speaking in high-pitched, feminine voices.

"Good luck!" one sang as he hugged the boy next to him.

"Thanks, sweetie," the other boy replied.

Sharp clapping interrupted their laughter; the group around me turned their heads. A man with short, tidy, steel–grey hair and black–rimmed glasses stood behind the counter. His dark suit and white shirt were accented by a black and red bowtie.

"Boys, boys, boys, is that any way to welcome a new student?" He shook his head to show he was annoyed. The boys sat down and I sighed with relief. Mabel was right about Uncle Malcolm.

Professor Jones looked down at me. "Miss Ross, I presume."

I smiled up at him. "Yes, sir."

Professor Jones scanned the room until his eyes rested on a particular student. "I do believe you have trouble seeing from the back, Mr. Young."

"Yes, sir," a voice replied.

Professor Jones looked down at me again and smiled. "I wonder if you would switch seats with him, Miss Ross."

"Sure." I stood up, collected my notebook, and headed toward the empty chair in the second last row of tables.

As I passed one of the students I heard, "You don't need a front seat—you won't be here long." There was a ripple of laughter and I felt my face grow hot. I sat down and opened my notebook.

The boy next to me leaned over and said, "Hi, I'm Jack."

Before I could reply, Professor Jones pointed at him. "You, sir!" he said. "What's your name?"

"Jack Stinson, sir."

"Take this seat in front of me before we have a tea party back there."

This time the boys' laughter was accompanied by desk banging and whistling. Professor Jones smiled and held up his hands until the boys quieted down. "I think we should ignore the obvious distraction and get down to work," he said. "What do I have in front of me?"

From somewhere in the room a voice replied, "An engine, sir."

My heart pounded in my ears. The voices in the room faded into the background. I took deep breaths and tried to figure out what had just happened. One minute Professor Jones was smiling at me. The next minute I was sitting at the back of the room and everyone was laughing at me. I couldn't imagine why Mabel called this man kind. He was her uncle, who treated her well, I got that—but was it possible no one had mentioned this other side of him over the years?

I felt a gentle touch on my back. "Don't turn around," a voice whispered. A few seconds passed and I heard, "Meet me at Frank's Coffee Shop on State Street after class." A slight nod was my answer.

My heart rate was almost back to normal and the voices around me grew in volume. Professor Jones was identifying the parts of the engine and the boys were taking notes. I looked down at my notebook and started to write. I wasn't listening to Professor Jones. Instead I listed all the parts of the car engine I'd seen at the airport yesterday. I added the function of each part as the rest of the class struggled to jot down everything Professor Jones said.

"Miss Ross!" I jumped and looked up. The class turned around to look at me.

"Am I going too fast for you?" Professor Jones asked.

"No, sir."

"Don't be afraid to ask me to slow down."

I nodded and looked down at my desk. The other students snickered and went back to taking notes. Finally, the class was over and Professor Jones wrote a homework assignment on the blackboard. I copied it into my notebook and stood up. Some students stopped to talk to Professor Jones but I hurried along the side aisle and out the door.

CHAPTER 7

NEW FRIENDS

———◄○►———

F ALLEN LEAVES CRUNCHED under my shoes on the walk back
to the Home Economics Building. I remembered that State
Street ran next to it. When I got to the corner, I didn't know
which way to turn. A girl at the trolley stop pointed left and
I thanked her.

It was another glorious fall day. I breathed in fresh air and
looked up into the clear blue sky. The sun felt warm on my
face. Ravens drifted on air currents high above. I took a few
more deep breaths before resuming my walk. In spite of what
had just happened in Professor Jones's class, I felt reassured
that the world outside was still functioning as it should.

Frank's Coffee Shop had a big front window with a door
beside it. I walked in to the smells of bacon, toast, and fresh
coffee. I hesitated at the counter but then spotted an empty
booth at the back. I slid across the green leather seat and
clasped my hands on the table. My stomach was still in a
knot when the waitress appeared. I knew I'd have trouble
swallowing anything but I had to order.

"Tea, please," I said.

"Coming right up," she said with a smile.

The door opened and a young man walked in. Since I was unsure who I was supposed to be meeting, I didn't try to catch his eye. He looked around until he spotted me in the back. With a wave, he headed in my direction. I thought he looked a bit like the boy from Cap's hangar, Matt Baker. They were both tall and slim with the same shade of blond hair and, as he came closer, the same blue eyes. The most noticeable difference between Matt and this boy was the way they walked. Matt strode across the hangar with an easy confidence but this boy moved as if he hadn't quite grown into his long legs yet.

He held out his hand when he reached my table. "Jamie Baker. I'm Matt's brother," he said.

I held out my hand and was surprised to see it trembling. If Jamie noticed, he pretended not to. He shook my hand firmly and sat down opposite me. I tried to say hello but my voice couldn't get past the lump in my throat. Seeing Jamie brought the whole classroom experience back.

"I understand you met my brother Matt at the airport," he said.

I nodded.

My tea arrived and Jamie poured it into a cup for me. He held up the small pitcher of milk. I nodded and he added some. He turned the teacup's handle toward me and smiled. As I sipped the soothing liquid, he began to speak.

"I'm so sorry you had to go through that," he said, shaking his head. "The man is just plain cruel."

A tear trickled down my cheek. I quickly wiped it away with the back of my hand. A few more sips of tea and I felt calmer. I smiled at Jamie and was about to thank him when an older boy walked up to our table. He put a hand on Jamie's shoulder.

"How's my little brother?"

"Eddie Elliott!" Jamie exclaimed. He jumped up and shook hands with the boy. He was as tall as Jamie but heavier set. His light brown, wavy hair was neatly combed and he wore a Purdue sweater over an open-necked shirt.

"This is Matt's best friend, Ed," Jamie told me. He sat down and pulled Ed down beside him. "Ed, this is my friend, Ginny Ross."

"So, *you're* Ginny Ross." Ed offered me his hand and we shook. "My dad said he wants to invite you to lunch when Amelia Earhart arrives. Apparently you know her?"

In response to Jamie's astonished look, I told him I would explain later. Ed asked a few questions about the Baker family while I sipped my tea and wondered if Ed's father was the president of the university. I turned my attention back to their conversation when I heard my name.

"Professor Jones gave Ginny a rough time this morning," Jamie was explaining. "And worse than that, he encouraged the other students to do the same."

Ed shook his head "I hope they didn't go along with him."

"Most did," Jamie replied. "How can he get away with that kind of behaviour?"

"He's already been in trouble for mistreating girls. But they always dropped out. Aside from being a misogynist, he's a good teacher."

"But I thought your dad was trying to attract more women to higher education," I pointed out.

Ed smiled when I made the connection with his name. "That's the one reason why Professor Jones may have to change his ways," he said.

We continued to talk about how I could survive his class. I certainly knew more about engines than most of the other students but Ed thought that fact might make Professor Jones more hostile.

"Maybe I should just keep a low profile, do the work, and get out of class as fast as I can," I suggested.

Jamie said he would be behind me all the way and we chuckled at his unintended pun. We ordered sandwiches and more tea because there was only one class that day. Some students wouldn't arrive until Monday, especially if they were involved in the harvest.

I slipped my hand into my pocket to make sure I had the American five-dollar bill Aunt Rose had given me before I left Harbour Grace. Because her hotel was still bringing in some money, she had paid for my train and ferry tickets. That five dollars was all I had to spend. With my change from lunch, I could finally pay Mabel back for the trolley ride.

After we finished eating, the three of us said goodbye outside the coffee shop. Before I walked back to the residence, Jamie gently took hold of my arm and asked about Amelia.

I showed him the four-leaf clover and repeated the story I'd told Mabel.

"Holy cow!" he said, as he gazed at the clover in his palm.

"But you can't tell anyone, if I want to keep a low profile," I reminded him.

"What about Matt?"

I thought for a second. "Do you think he can he keep a secret?"

"You bet."

I agreed and we walked to the Women's Residence together. There was something I didn't share with Jamie—Mabel's description of her uncle. The Professor Jones we knew and the Uncle Malcolm she knew seemed like two different people.

At the front steps, I thanked Jamie for his support and headed inside. Mabel jumped up from her desk when I opened the door. "Where have you been?" she asked. "I was afraid you got lost."

I sat down on my bed and she joined me. "Sorry you were worried. I had lunch with some engineering friends."

"How was Uncle Malcolm's class?"

I hesitated before I spoke. Mabel had described him in such a positive way; I had to be careful not to offend her. She was the friend who'd rescued me at the train station, my roommate. It was important for me to choose my words carefully.

"Well, at first he was friendly," I started.

Mabel nodded. "I told you so."

I cleared my throat. "But as the class went on, I didn't feel so...welcome."

"What do you mean?"

"A boy couldn't see from the back so your uncle gave him my front seat."

"What's wrong with that?"

"Nothing, I guess. But when the boy next to me leaned over to say hi, your uncle moved him away from me."

"He is strict. I'll give you that," Mabel said, standing up. "My class was great! A lot of the girls from residence were there but something odd happened. Girls I've never met seemed to know my name. Others whispered as I walked by."

"You and I were at registration together," I replied. "I hope you're not being singled out because you're my friend. You know the old saying: you're judged by the company you keep."

"Hey, don't worry about me," Mabel said. "I grew up with two older brothers. I'm a lot tougher than I look!" She stood up and flexed her muscles, just as Elizabeth walked in.

"Have you done your food science homework yet?" she asked. Mabel said yes and they walked over to her desk together.

My mind went back to Professor Jones's class. The way Mabel explained her uncle's behaviour made me doubt what I'd seen, heard, and felt. Was I overreacting to what happened? Maybe he was just teasing me and I had taken it the wrong way.

On the other hand, Jamie confirmed that Professor Jones had been cruel in the past and Ed confirmed he had the reputation of mistreating girls. I couldn't have been overreacting.

No matter how hard I tried to figure out what had actually happened in class, I was still confused. There was only one thing I was sure of—the feeling of fear in the pit of my stomach.

CHAPTER 8

OLD FRIEND

—◄○►—

B Y THE NEXT week, all classes were running on schedule. That meant I would see Professor Jones again. But at least I'd formed a plan—lay low, do my work, and leave the classroom as fast as I could.

"Are you sure you don't want me to show you the way again?" Mabel asked.

"I remember how to get there, but thanks." I waved goodbye to Mabel, Elizabeth, and Barb before heading toward the Mechanical Engineering Building.

I was early enough to avoid the boys on the front steps. But when I opened the main door, my stomach began to churn. *Stay calm. Deep breaths.* I walked quickly down the hallway and into room 132. *Empty. Good.* I sat down and waited.

Jamie Baker came in, smiled at me, and slipped into his seat. "Whatever you do, don't turn around. If Professor Jones suspects we're friends, he'll move me."

I smiled and whispered over my shoulder, "Message received. Over and out."

The door opened and a few more boys walked in. They quietly took their seats. One of them was Jack Stinson, who had been moved away from me last week. The boys from the front steps came in next. They smiled and walked toward me.

Jack stood up, tucked his tie into the front of his shirt, and blocked their way. "Why don't you four act your age?" he said. "In case you haven't noticed, this isn't a kindergarten class."

"Well, well, if it isn't a knight in shining armour!" one of them said.

Jack pointed his finger. "One more word from any of you and you'll be eating a knuckle sandwich." The boys looked at each other and sat down.

Jack didn't look like someone you wanted to annoy. He was tall and dark haired, with piercing brown eyes. Where the Baker boys were slim, Jack was broad shouldered and solid. He looked perfectly capable of delivering a knuckle sandwich.

I felt a gentle tap on my shoulder but knew not to turn around. "Jack has three younger sisters," Jamie whispered. I nodded to show I heard him.

The class slowly filled up until Professor Jones arrived.

"Good morning, gentlemen. You know the parts of an engine and their function. Let's look at the process called internal combustion." All of that was said without a glance in my direction.

As I had done in the previous class, I wrote my own notes. I had demonstrated internal combustion to Cap when I serviced the Taylor Cub. I quickly finished but kept my pen in my hand and my eyes on my notebook.

"You're not writing," Jamie whispered. I moved to one side to let him see my notes.

"You, sir!" Professor Jones shouted. "What's your name?"

"Jamie Baker, sir."

"Are you and Miss Ross writing love notes back there?" He smiled with the same look a spider gives a fly he's caught in his web.

Jamie's "No, sir" could hardly be heard over the hooting and laughing.

"Let's share that message with the class. Bring your book up here, Miss Ross." The boys clapped and shouted.

As I walked to the front of the class, I could feel every eye burning into my back. I laid my notebook on the counter and turned it toward Professor Jones. He read for a few seconds. "So, you do know something about engines," he whispered.

"Yes, sir." I kept my eyes on my book so he couldn't see the heat I was feeling on my face.

He looked up at the class. "I'll let you off this time," he said in a loud voice. "But don't let it happen again."

"Read it! Read it!" the boys chanted.

Professor Jones held up his hands and smiled. "Next time, gentlemen." He waved me back to my seat.

I sat down and closed my eyes. How could I be so stupid? This was not the way to keep a low profile. Worse than that, I'd revealed much more about myself than I'd planned. Now that he knew I understood engines, he might feel more threatened than if he thought I knew nothing.

Jamie caught up with me after class. "I'm so sorry. I shouldn't have spoken to you."

"It's not your fault. Professor Jones doesn't need an excuse to humiliate me."

We walked to Frank's Coffee Shop and joined Matt and Ed.

I explained what happened in class. "I'm just plain stupid." I hit my forehead with my fist.

"Wait a minute." Matt grabbed my hand in mid-air. "Why are *you* stupid?"

"My plan was to keep a low profile!"

"I'm not so sure that's what you should be doing."

"What do you mean?" I asked.

"You need to show Professor Jones what you can do," Matt replied. "Make it hard for him to pretend you don't know anything. As for the rest of the class, the boys may not like being shown up by a girl but they'll know you have the right to be there."

"Maybe that is a better idea." Ed looked at me. "Fight back, or he'll bury you."

I put my hands over my face and saw Mom and me standing in our family store again. We had been at odds for years over my plan to become a pilot. But in those years, I'd come to know what to do. Stay out of slapping distance. Gauge the level of her anger. Decide when to push the issue and when to let it drop. I finally won the battle because I knew her so well.

But this wasn't Harbour Grace and Professor Jones wasn't Mom. Standing up to him could backfire but what choice did I have? I dropped my hands onto my lap and took a deep breath.

"You're right. I have to fight back. I just hope I'm up to the challenge."

"We'll help you," Matt said, and Ed agreed.

———◦———

That afternoon, I met my English professor, Professor Weeks. No one was more different from Professor Jones. He treated every student with the same courtesy and respect. Whenever I raised my hand, he called on me. Aside from Jamie, Jack, and a few others, the boys obviously considered English a waste of time. Most gazed out the window or finished Professor Jones's engineering homework.

After class, I arrived back at the women's residence at the same time as Mabel. I'd been working on what to say to her about her supposedly kind uncle, when Elizabeth came down the front steps.

"There's a note taped to your door," she said.

I ran up the stairs and Mabel followed. The envelope had my name written in black ink. I tore it off the door. "It's from Amelia!" I whispered. "I know her handwriting." My hands were shaking so badly, I had trouble opening the envelope. I pulled out the letter and started to read out loud.

"Dear Ginny—"

"Not here!" Mabel hissed. She opened the door and pulled me in. "Okay. Now you can read it."

> *Dear Ginny,*
>
> *I arrived at Purdue today—in my new Lockheed Electra 10E. You're going to love it! I've been in discussions all day with President Elliott and I'm having dinner at his house this evening. After that we have a meeting with the Board of Trustees. My official duties start tomorrow, so I'll see you at those. I don't know how often we'll be able to meet alone with the schedule they've given me but I'll do my best.*
>
> *Your friend, Amelia*

I held the letter to my chest and sank onto my bed.

"Wow!" Mabel said. "You really *do* know Amelia Earhart!"

I laughed and replied, "That's what I've been trying to tell you!"

"And you'll introduce me to her?"

"Of course!" After everything Mabel had done for me, I was happy to be able to do something for her.

CHAPTER 9

AMELIA

———◄○►———

THE NEXT MORNING, I sat down for breakfast with my friends from the second floor. I said good morning but no one answered. Someone at another table had all their attention. My heart jumped when I saw Amelia—her tousled blonde hair, her gap-toothed smile, and her trousers. She sat with our residence director, Miss Schleman, and Miss Stratton, Dean of Women.

Without moving her gaze, Sarah whispered, "Amelia is so pretty."

"Did you see how tall she is?" Elizabeth asked.

"I wish we could wear trousers," Barb added. "They look so comfortable."

I cleared my throat loudly. "Did it ever occur to you lot that Amelia might like to eat her breakfast in peace?"

They turned around and looked at me. One by one they agreed and continued eating.

"Aren't you excited?" Joanne asked.

"Of course," I replied. "I just think she could use a little space."

"Tell that to the seniors." Joan pointed to the table closest to Amelia. Everyone was practically leaning out of her chair to get a better view.

The three women stood up at the same time and pushed in their chairs. Miss Schleman held up her hand until the dining room was quiet.

"I'd like to introduce our special guest for the next few weeks. Miss Amelia Earhart has kindly agreed to join our staff as a part-time counsellor for women and aviation advisor. While she's here she will be living in our guest suite on the first floor." Miss Schleman turned to Amelia and asked if she would like to say a few words.

"Thank you, Miss Schleman," Amelia said as she scanned the room. She caught my eye and smiled. "It's a pleasure to be here at Purdue and to see so many enthusiastic young women. I'm looking forward to our work together. I'd like to begin by inviting all of you to a presentation this evening, in the living room at seven o'clock. Miss Schleman thinks you'd like to hear about my transatlantic flight."

We all stood up and clapped loudly. Amelia smiled and gave us a quick wave before she and the other two ladies walked toward the door. When she got to our table, Amelia stopped and squeezed my hands. "Ginny Ross from Harbour Grace, Newfoundland! I can't believe how you've changed."

"I'm not the twelve-year-old girl you met on that rainy day in Rye."

Amelia laughed. "You definitely are not! You've lost your drowned-cat look."

I laughed too and then turned to Mabel. "Amelia, this is my roommate, Mabel Anderson, and the others are my neighbours on the second floor."

Amelia shook hands with Mabel. "It's a pleasure to meet you, Mabel."

"The pleasure is all mine, Miss Earhart."

Amelia gave the rest of the girls a cheery wave. "Hopefully I'll see all of you at seven tonight."

"Definitely!" Mabel replied while the others nodded enthusiastically.

Amelia turned and followed Miss Schleman and Miss Stratton out the door. There was complete silence for a few seconds. Then the room erupted.

"How do you know Amelia Earhart?"

"Where did you meet her?"

"What's she like?"

Everyone sat down and looked at me expectantly.

"Tell them about Amelia in Harbour Grace," Mabel suggested.

I stood up and rested my hands on the back of my chair while I spoke. I described Amelia's landing, but decided to leave out the part about helping her. I didn't want to sound as if I was bragging. The girls continued asking questions until it was time for us to go to class.

As we did every morning, those of us from the second floor left the dining room together. We continued out the front door and along the sidewalk toward the Home Economics Building. I answered more questions before I had to head in the opposite direction.

"I have to get to class early today," I explained. Mabel can give you more details about Amelia and me." I waved and headed toward the Physics Building, where I was about to meet a new professor.

The front steps were empty when I got there. A good sign. I opened the door, walked into the smell of floor wax, hurried along the hall, and up the stairs. I opened my notebook and checked my class schedule—room 254 with Professor Abernathy. I stood outside the classroom for a minute or two and then entered.

A man with white hair was seated at a counter at the front of the room. He stood up and smiled when I entered. I tried to gauge his attitude toward having a girl in his class. His smile looked friendly, but I'd fallen for that before.

"Professor Abernathy," he held out his hand and I shook it. "You must be Miss Ross."

"I'm afraid so."

"May I presume you've met Professor Jones?"

"That man is some hard ticket," I blurted out. I quickly covered my mouth with my hand.

Professor Abernathy chuckled. "Ah, yes." He gestured toward a seat at the front of the room. I sat down and he joined me. "Captain Aretz tells me your uncle Harry has taught you a great deal about engines," he continued. "What do you know about navigation?"

A group of boys were roughhousing as they came into the room but as soon as they saw Professor Abernathy, they came to a halt.

"Please leave and enter only when you can do so as gentlemen," he told them. Then he turned back to me. "You were saying?"

"Uncle Harry taught me quite a lot about navigation, especially celestial navigation."

Professor Abernathy smiled. "Then we shall be great friends." He stood up and walked behind the counter at the front of the room. The same group of boys came in quietly and sat down. He smiled at them and said, "Thank you, gentlemen."

Others entered slowly and took seats behind me, until the room was almost full. I recognized the boys who had leaned into my face and shouted at me in Professor Jones's class. When they walked through the door, a steely gaze from Professor Abernathy met them. He didn't break eye contact until they had settled quietly in their seats. *How does he know they're troublemakers*, I wondered?

Instead of diving into a lesson, Professor Abernathy asked a lot of questions: where were we from, did we have siblings at Purdue, who had driven a car, had anyone flown in a plane? A few students raised their hands to the last question but I decided not to. Professor Abernathy glanced at me but said nothing. I was quite sure Cap had told him about my flight, but somehow, he knew not to mention it here.

He passed around a seating plan for us to fill in. "Please stay in the seat you currently hold until I have learned your names.

Then you may sit wherever you wish." I wasn't moving. Jack shared my table, and Jamie sat behind us.

Professor Abernathy concluded the class by asking each of us to jot down what we thought might be discussed in physics. "Do some brainstorming before our next class," he said. Then he dismissed us. The boys filed out respectfully.

I stood up, gathered my books, and approached Professor Abernathy. "Thank you for making me feel so comfortable, sir."

"But of course, my dear!" he said. "I'm happy to have you in my class."

I walked straight back to the residence and told Mabel about the wonderful class I'd had. We stretched out on our beds and talked more about Amelia. I felt lucky to have Mabel in my life but there was something about our friendship that kept niggling in the back of my mind.

I couldn't introduce Mabel to my other friends. Jamie, Jack, and Ed knew Professor Jones. But Mabel knew Uncle Malcolm.

I felt like I was leading a double life and I didn't know what to do about it.

CHAPTER 10

ATLANTIC FLIGHT

———◄○►———

AMELIA SAT WITH the seniors at dinner. I noticed how many of them were drinking buttermilk. They must have heard Amelia asking for it at breakfast. She waved to Mabel and me but stayed where she was.

Our table of girls from the second floor wanted to hear more about Harbour Grace, the airstrip, and my family. They said they'd enjoyed Mabel's stories but wanted to know more.

"Tell them about the first time you met Amelia, when you ran away from home."

"You told them that?"

"You didn't tell me not to!"

I smiled at Mabel and shook my head.

"Go on then," she urged.

"I suppose the most memorable event, besides meeting Amelia, was the mugging."

"You got *mugged*?" Joanne asked, her fork stopped halfway to her mouth.

I nodded. "In Boston, on a deserted back street, a man held me up at knifepoint. I made the mistake of putting all my money in my boot so I lost it all at once. Apparently, I should have put it in two or three different places."

"Mabel said you were twelve when you ran away," Joan said. "Weren't you afraid to travel alone?"

"At that age, I didn't realize what could happen. I had to find Amelia and that's all I thought about. Now I'm more aware of what can go wrong. In fact, I sometimes think I was braver then than I am now."

This sparked a lively discussion around the table. Some girls felt the same as me, while others felt they got braver as they got older. Then the conversation drifted back to Amelia and me. I continued to answer their questions and to describe other flights from Harbour Grace. They laughed out loud when I told them one pilot had named his dog Tailwind.

I glanced over at Mabel and smiled. This was such a pleasant change from all the negative comments at registration and in Professor Jones's class. At this table there was nothing but acceptance. Sure, some of the girls might have been a little jealous but no one showed it. And for that, I was grateful.

Before we filed out of the dining room, Miss Schleman reminded us about Amelia's presentation that evening. As if anyone had forgotten.

————◦————

Just before seven, Mabel and I walked downstairs. The living room held lots of sofas and chairs but we knew there would be a rush for seats. We lined up at the door where two seniors, Alice Edwards and Cecilia Hofmeister, were supervising the seating. Alice was taking her job very seriously. "Seniors first!" she shouted down the line.

"We don't mind waiting our turn," I replied. Mabel and I stepped to one side just as Miss Schleman and Amelia walked into the foyer.

For the presentation, Amelia wore a navy blue suit with a skirt instead of trousers. A white blouse and flat-heeled black shoes finished her outfit. I wondered how many seniors would be shopping for navy blue suits over the next few days.

When she passed us, Amelia leaned over and whispered to me. The girls who noticed nudged each other and smiled. Although I told myself I wasn't interested in praise or acknowledgment, the truth was Amelia's special treatment gave me a warm feeling.

"What did Amelia say?" Mabel whispered.

"She said we'd talk soon."

Mabel squeezed my hand and we walked to the back of the line.

All the seniors, sophomores, and juniors were seated before Alice and Cecilia finally allowed the freshmen in. Every sofa, chair, and footstool was filled, as well as the extra chairs that had been brought in from the dining room. Mabel, our friends, and I sat on the floor directly in front of Amelia. It was the only space available in the whole room.

Miss Schleman stood up and waited until we were quiet. She introduced Amelia and we responded with thunderous applause.

Amelia stood up and smiled until the noise died down. She began by describing all the preparation that went into a transatlantic flight. She told us about Harbour Grace, including her meetings with Uncle Harry, Aunt Rose, and me. A few of the freshmen smiled at me and I smiled back. Again, I got that warm feeling. Instead of being an oddity, I was an accepted pilot-in-training...at least in here.

After a brief account of her flight, Amelia asked for questions from the audience.

"Was flying over the ocean frightening?" the girl sitting next to Alice asked.

"You bet!" Amelia replied. "After the first hour the altimeter failed."

"The what?" a girl from the nearest sofa asked.

"The altimeter measures the distance from the plane to the ground—in this case, it was the ocean."

Amelia paused to allow the concerned murmurs to die down. Then she described the next few hours. The visibility was good and she could see how far above the waves she was flying. But after three hours, she could smell burning oil. Through the windshield, she saw a small blue flame licking through a broken weld.

There was complete silence in the room.

"Is that serious?" Mabel asked.

"It certainly can be."

"Why didn't you turn around?" a girl in one of the easy chairs asked.

"The airport at Harbour Grace wasn't lit at night and I still had a heavy load of gasoline. I thought it would be safer to go on."

"Surely that was the end of your problems," the same girl said. She was leaning forward with her elbows on her knees.

Every girl in the room waited for Amelia's answer. A few sat on the edges of their seats and Alice's mouth hung open. Although I knew the story, I felt my heart pounding as I listened.

Amelia explained the events of the next four hours. She found herself in a rainstorm. Then the rain on the windshield turned to ice. The controls froze and the plane went into a spin. She managed to pull out of it by talking through the recovery steps she'd been taught.

"Luckily I gained control, but I was awfully close to the whitecaps," she said. "At least the warmer air melted the ice."

"Did you stay that close to the ocean for the rest of the trip?" asked a girl sitting at Amelia's feet.

"I flew higher until I iced up and then lower to melt the ice. This went on for some hours."

"I hope *that* was the end of your problems!" Mabel said. She was now sitting up on her knees.

"There was just one more, Mabel," Amelia replied. "I turned on the reserve gas tank to find the cockpit gauge was broken. Gasoline started trickling down the side of my neck."

"What about the flames outside the windshield?"

"They had me worried, that's for sure, but there was nothing I could do to change the situation. I just had to carry on. Finally, on one of my drops to sea level, I saw a small fishing boat. I knew from its size it couldn't be far from the coast, probably Ireland. When I saw railway tracks, I followed them until I saw a pasture. The landing was a bit bumpy but otherwise easy."

"Were you in Ireland?" asked another girl.

"Yes, Culmore is near Londonderry in northwestern Ireland." The whole room seemed to sigh with relief.

"I hope you're not going to suggest that I could become a pilot," Mabel said. "I prefer a quiet life. No crashing into the North Atlantic for me!"

Amelia smiled. "Ginny is probably the only other person in the room who shares my passion for flying. But I would encourage you to find your own dream and not just settle for what others expect you to do. If you want a traditional, quiet life, that's fine. Just make sure you know what your options are."

When the questions ended, Miss Schleman thanked Amelia. We all stood up, applauded loudly, and surrounded Amelia to shake her hand. Mabel and I inched our way forward. If Amelia didn't have time to talk then, maybe she would arrange to meet us later.

There were only two girls ahead of us when Miss Schleman stepped in. "Sorry, ladies," she said. "Amelia is due at a reception with the university trustees. I'm afraid I have to get her there right now."

Amelia smiled at those of us who were still waiting. "Another time," she said.

I gave her a wave. She was busy, I understood that, but I still felt a twinge of disappointment. I longed to tell her how much I loved being at Purdue, in spite of the scary classes with Professor Jones. If I could tell her about my problems with him, maybe she could suggest ways to solve them.

Mabel supported me because we were friends. Matt, Cap, Jamie, and Jack supported me because they knew I was good with engines. But I wanted Amelia to reassure me that everything would be all right.

CHAPTER 11

TRUTH

———◆◇◆———

THE HEAT MABEL and I had felt at the train station was gone. There was a chill in the air. We wore skirts and jackets instead of flowered cotton dresses. Mabel kicked the dry leaves as we walked to class.

"I miss seeing Amelia at the residence," she said.

"Here, hold my books and I'll tell you what she's been doing." I took Amelia's schedule out of my pocket. "She spoke to the girls in the Mortar Board Society at a luncheon, the boys in East Cary Hall at a dinner, and the boys in the Iron Key Society at another dinner. Then we shook hands with her at the Women's Self-Government Association and Student Senate Reception."

"What's next?" Mabel asked.

"She's the guest speaker at a special convocation, tomorrow at eight o'clock."

"When does she start her student conferences?"

I looked at the schedule again. "Not until next week. She speaks to the senior girls in small groups during the day, then to the whole group in the evening. We're freshmen so we'll see her last." I put the schedule back in my pocket and reached for my books.

"Convocation will be interesting," Mabel said, "but it's not the same as sitting on the floor in front of her and listening to her adventures,"

"That's true. But I just like having her close by." The truth was I still hoped for the opportunity to speak with Amelia privately.

When we reached the Home Economics Building, Mabel stopped and told me to have a good day. I walked backwards and waved. "You too."

I was less frightened than usual about Professor Jones's class that day. Since I'd talked to the boys, I had a new plan. I would show him what I knew and prove that I had the right to be there. I took my seat at the back and waited.

Professor Jones walked in, stepped behind the counter at the front, and said a cheerful "Good morning, gentlemen."

He asked a few questions but I didn't raise my hand. I was waiting for one that the boys didn't know. Professor Jones would have no choice but to call on me.

"Why does a float fail to operate properly?" he asked.

No hands went up. I raised mine but instead of calling on me, Professor Jones gave the answer himself. The next time I raised my hand, I waved it so everyone could see. Again, Professor Jones gave the answer. I decided to try once more. When no one else put up his hand, I waved mine even harder.

"Are there flies back there, Miss Ross?"

I lowered my hand. "No, sir."

"Then kindly stop waving."

The boys snickered.

"But I know the answer."

"You will know the answer when I call on you."

So much for showing him what I knew.

As soon as the class was over, I left. Apparently, it was back to the drawing board for plan number three.

———◆———

The next day was Saturday. We headed to the airport because Amelia's Electra 10E was in the hangar. The mechanical and aeronautical engineering students had been invited to drop in and see it. I invited Mabel to come along.

Amelia stood with Cap and another man, examining the engine. As soon as she saw us, she walked over. She gave me a hug and Mabel a handshake.

"Come and have a closer look," she beckoned.

We followed her to the large silver plane, with its twin engines. A wooden scaffold stood next to it.

"The board of trustees is coming to see the Electra and speak to me about my flying laboratory," Amelia explained.

Cap greeted us and then Amelia introduced us to her mechanic, Bo McKneely.

"I'd shake your hands," he said, "but I don't want to share this grease."

"Ginny wouldn't mind," Cap replied with a chuckle. He waved us closer.

"In that case, I'll explain what this beauty can do," Bo said. "The Electra 10E has two Wasp engines, rated at 550 horsepower each. This plane can fly to an altitude of 19,000 feet and has a range of 4,000 miles." We nodded while he spoke and I concluded Amelia's next flight would be a long one.

Cap invited us to see the cockpit. We climbed the scaffold and looked into a compact space with two seats. I wondered if Amelia was taking a co-pilot with her. Cap called up to tell us there was room in the back for a navigator. "This is going to be a very long flight," I whispered to Mabel. "She has already crossed the Atlantic alone so if she's taking a navigator, she must be going a lot farther."

As we came down the steps, Matt walked over. "The Electra is really something, isn't it?"

"Amazing," I agreed, turning back to gaze at its silver fuselage.

Amelia joined us and I introduced her to Matt. They shook hands and Amelia told him she was happy to hear he was training to be a pilot. She said he and I were just the right age to take over when she decided to retire.

"That won't be for a long time," Matt said.

"I feel like I have one more long flight in me," Amelia replied. "Then I'll be ready to settle down. I'll still be involved in aviation, but in a different way."

Just as she was about to say something else, the trustees walked into the hangar. Amelia excused herself to join Cap and Bo.

"She's very easy to talk to," Matt said. "Thanks for the introduction!"

He, Mabel, and I walked to one of the workbenches on the opposite side of the hangar. "Jamie told me what happened in class yesterday," Matt said.

"Ah…." I didn't know how to answer. I hadn't told him that Mabel was Professor Jones's niece. Before I could think of a way to stop him from talking, he continued.

"I don't know what it will take to get that man off your back," he said.

"Who?" Mabel asked.

"Professor Jones," Matt replied.

I felt my face burning. Mabel's eyes were on me. I looked away while my mind raced for something to say.

"What did you tell Matt?" Mabel demanded.

"Nothing, I—"

"Nothing?" Mabel's voice was rising. She looked anxiously toward the crowd around Amelia, glanced at Matt, and headed for the door.

"Mabel!" I ran and caught up to her outside the hangar. "I'm sorry you had to hear about your uncle that way…but I didn't say anything to Matt. His brother, Jamie, is in my class."

"So?"

"Well…." I tried to put it delicately but the words wouldn't come. "Mabel, the whole class knows your uncle is trying to force me to drop out."

"He would never do that. In all the time I've known him, he's been kind and generous. Not just to me but to all his students. The boys certainly like and respect him."

"But I'm not a boy. So he doesn't want me in engineering."

"That's not true."

"I understand why you can't accept it."

"Accept what?"

"That your uncle Malcolm is making my life miserable."

"I don't accept it because it's not true." Mabel swung around and walked away.

I followed until she shouted over her shoulder, "Go away, Ginny! I don't want to talk to you anymore."

I stood frozen for a few seconds wondering what to do next. My feet were itching to follow her but my brain said, *Give her time to cool off.* I couldn't believe this was happening. I'd been so careful to keep Mabel away from Jamie, Jack, and Ed, I'd forgotten to mention "Uncle Malcolm" to Matt. How could I have been so careless? Mabel had always been there for me, and this was how I repaid her! My whole body felt numb, as I walked slowly back to the hangar.

Matt was waiting for me by the door so I explained that Professor Jones was Mabel's uncle.

He shook his head. "I'm so sorry."

I sighed. "At least the truth is out."

Jamie approached us. "A girl just ran past me in tears."

"Mabel is my roommate—and Professor Jones's niece."

"That must be awkward," Jamie said. "What are you going to do?"

"I wish I knew."

Jamie told us he was on his way to the coffee shop to meet Ed. Matt asked me to help him finish servicing a Taylor Cub and then we could join them. I promised to come back to the hangar as soon as I checked on Mabel.

Back at the residence, I looked in our room, the living room, the dining room, the kitchen, the laundry room, and the recreation room in the basement. I asked everyone if they'd seen Mabel but the answer was always no.

I returned to the empty living room and slumped down on one of the sofas. How could I have let this happen after everything Mabel had done for me? I brushed a tear off my cheek and, with a sigh, stood up and returned to the hangar.

I told Matt that my search had been unsuccessful. He thought Mabel just needed some time to cool off but I didn't think it was that simple. For the time being, I couldn't think of what else to do so I helped him finish his work on the plane. Our hands moved automatically, as if we were playing a piano duet. Each of us knew the other's next move.

After we washed our hands, Cap joined us and made notes on his clipboard. "I assume you worked with Ginny."

"Yes, sir."

Cap smiled and looked at me. "I hope he did his share."

Matt blushed. "I forgot to check the float—again!"

"But Ginny reminded you."

Matt's blush deepened.

"Off you go," Cap said with a smile. He waved as we left the hangar.

"Let's go for a root beer," Matt suggested. "It will help get your mind off Mabel, at least for a little while."

I knew nothing could get my mind off Mabel but there was an important question I wanted to ask Ed. At the coffee shop, I sat on the bench beside him and Matt slid in next to Jamie. When the waitress came over, Matt ordered two root beers. Jamie told us Ed had just been explaining why Professor Jones got away with treating female students so badly.

"He's a tenured professor, which means he can't be fired unless he does something to blacken the good name of Purdue. The boys like him, so his teaching reviews are always very good. He cooperates well with the other engineering professors and Dean Potter likes him."

I had been wondering if one professor could prevent a student's overall success. Ed had been at Purdue the longest so he was probably the best one to ask.

"If I fail Professor Jones's class, do I fail my whole year?"

"I'm afraid so," Ed replied. His classwork and his shops are compulsory subjects. That's why you need a minimum of 65 percent to advance to the next semester."

"Ginny can get the marks. That's no problem," Jamie said. "But how can she survive his mistreatment?"

Ed thought for a few seconds. "Maybe we should review what I said before."

"Stand up to him or he'll bury me?" I asked.

Ed cringed and admitted it probably wasn't such good advice, given the circumstances. Matt said he was reconsidering what he'd said, too. If I made Professor Jones angry, my situation would only get worse.

"So, what can I do?"

"Maybe you should go back to your original plan for now," Ed replied. "Lay low and do your work. The exams are in a couple of weeks, and if you do well, he'll have to give you a good mark."

"Stand first in our class," Jamie said. "That will show everyone you belong there."

"Should I still raise my hand?"

"Occasionally," Ed replied. "Just don't wave it around."

"You mean don't wave a red cape in front of a charging bull?" I asked.

The boys laughed and Ed stood up. He had to get home because his dad was hosting Amelia and a few others for dinner.

Matt and Jamie walked me back to the residence. I searched all the same places, with no luck. Back on the front steps, I told them Mabel still wasn't there. They told me not to worry. She'd come home when she was ready.

Not worrying was easier said than done, especially when some of the girls asked where Mabel was at dinner. "She's probably at her uncle's," Joanne offered. "He pays her to clean his den because he doesn't trust anyone else with his papers." They all agreed and the butterflies in my stomach calmed down temporarily.

As soon as I could, I returned to our room to do homework.

But my brain just wouldn't work. After every few lines of reading, Mabel's face crept into my mind—her face and some act of kindness. "I'll pay for both of us," she'd said at the trolley stop, "and you can pay me back."

Hours passed before Mabel came in. I was already in bed when she walked quietly into our darkened room and closed the door behind her. I sat up but didn't turn on the light.

"Where have you been? I've been worried about you."

There was no answer.

CHAPTER 12

CONVOCATION

———◀o▶———

M<small>ABEL WAS HER</small> old self at breakfast the next morning... at least with the other girls. She still wasn't speaking to me. If the others noticed, they didn't mention it. All the talk was about Convocation. Some of the seniors mentioned wearing suits, hats, and gloves. But we freshmen decided school clothes would be fine for us.

I left Mabel and the second-floor girls at the Home Economics Building and headed to the Michael Golden Shops. The buildings were just behind mechanical engineering so I knew my way. This was the practical part of Professor Jones's class, but I wasn't worried. This was the hands-on world of engines—my world.

Back home, I would head for the Archibald Hotel every day after school. The smell of the sea was strong along Water Street. The fishermen shouted hello to me from the town wharf and I waved back but didn't stop. Uncle Harry was waiting for me in the garage behind the hotel, where we worked on Aunt Rose's model T Ford. I couldn't help smiling when I remembered the way he talked to me.

"You're some smart, so you are. Most men don't know how to gap spark plugs."

"Most men don't have cars," I replied with a grin.

"Well, even if they did, you'd still put them to shame!"

I walked up the front steps with confidence and opened the door. Instead of tables, workbenches stood around the room. On each was a small engine. They didn't look like automobile engines. In fact, some of them were much larger.

Jamie ambled in and I smiled at the image of a baby giraffe that flashed into my mind.

"I knew I'd find you here," he said, setting his books down. "How's Mabel?"

"She won't speak to me. I invited her to Convocation with us, but she ignored me."

Jack walked in next and joined us. "Sorry to hear about Mabel," he said. "Jamie told me what happened. Maybe she just needs time to realize what her uncle is really like."

I explained that Mabel's uncle had always been kind to her—and that he was paying her tuition. She didn't know the Professor Jones we knew.

"You're in a tough situation," Jack said.

"I know." What I didn't know was how I could've been so stupid. If I'd told Matt about Mabel's uncle Malcolm, none of this would have happened. *Dumb, dumb, dumb*, I told myself.

We'd been walking around the room while we talked. Jamie asked what kind of engines were on the workbenches but Jack and I just shrugged. We examined ours but that didn't help. More boys arrived and stood in threes around the other engines.

Finally, someone said, "I think this one is from a tractor."

The door opened and Professor Jones entered, wearing a navy blue lab coat. It was buttoned, but his white collar and red bowtie remained visible. "All right, gentlemen. Let's get started. Who can tell me what this is?"

The boy who guessed spoke again: "A tractor engine?"

"Yours is a John Deere. But there is a different engine in front of each group. I want you to examine your engine and explain to the rest of the class how internal combustion takes place."

"We're in luck," Jamie whispered. "Ginny did this at the hangar for Matt and Cap Aretz."

Jack smiled and declared he'd joined the right group. He tucked his tie into the front of his shirt. Then he and Jamie looked around the engine while I explained the process.

"Afraid to get your hands dirty, Miss Ross?" came Professor Jones's voice as he approached our workbench.

I stayed calm and didn't take his bait. "No, sir."

"Then let's have you remove some of those parts so we can have a better look."

"Sure."

I removed the breather, the manifold covers, and the carburetor. My sleeves got greasy and my nails were black.

But I didn't care. I explained everything I was doing to Jack and Jamie.

"Hmmph," Professor Jones said before he walked away.

After half an hour, it was time for the presentations. Some of the boys had trouble applying what they'd learned in the classroom to the actual engines. In those cases, Professor Jones helped them. Jack and Jamie decided I should present the information, just to be on the safe side.

When our turn came I said, "This engine is—"

"Excuse me, Miss Ross," Professor Jones interrupted. "Let's see if Mr. Stinson can speak for himself. He seemed rather eager to join your group."

Jack repeated what I had told them. He didn't need any help, but all he got from Professor Jones was a dirty look.

We left class together and walked in the direction of the Women's Residence.

"Thanks for your help, Ginny," Jack said. "You explained that process so well, old Professor Jones should be worried about his job."

I smiled because I knew Jack was trying to cheer me up, but the truth was all I could think about was Mabel. Our conversation turned to Convocation and we agreed to sit together. I wondered if I would have the courage to ask Mabel to join us again.

My strategy so far had been to leave the Uncle Malcolm issue alone. I didn't want to make matters worse by forcing Mabel to talk about it before she was ready. The waiting created a queasiness in my stomach that never went away.

———◄○►———

At seven o'clock, I stood outside the Memorial Gymnasium. I couldn't help smiling when I saw the boys walking toward me. Seeing them from a distance made their differences more obvious. Jack strode confidently, while loose-limbed Jamie loped along beside him. They both smiled and waved when they saw me.

"Mabel still ignoring you?" Jamie asked.

"I'm afraid so."

"Is she coming by herself?" Jack wanted to know.

"I don't know, but I hope she doesn't miss seeing Amelia."

Then Jack and I followed Jamie down the centre aisle. "This will give us the best view of the stage," he said, leading us to the middle of the row. We sat down.

Ed and Matt joined us at seven thirty. The ceremony didn't start until nine, but we knew seats would go quickly. We chatted about Amelia while we waited, and I asked Ed how dinner had gone at his house.

"Amelia is a real lady," he said. "A very interesting lady." He explained the dinner was intended to support female professors who felt ignored at Purdue. Even though they taught home economics or physical education, Amelia came up with good suggestions to make them feel more valued at the male-dominated university. "She's knowledgeable about more than aviation," Ed said.

I turned to Jamie. "What did she say when she spoke at East Cary Hall?"

"She set a few students and professors back on their heels," he replied. "She pointed out that women have as much right to pursue careers outside the home as men. A woman can get married *after* she's had some life of her own."

"One boy said he was having enough trouble finding a girlfriend without Amelia encouraging them to delay marriage." Matt demonstrated the boy's hopeless expression and we all laughed.

The room filled up quickly. Seats were held for students and faculty members until 7:55, and then were opened to the public at no charge. I kept looking for Mabel but couldn't find her in the crowd.

By nine, all 3,500 seats were filled. Mrs. Virginia C. Meredith, the only woman member of the University Board of Trustees, walked onto the stage. She stood for a moment while the gymnasium quieted. Then she introduced Amelia. She noted Amelia's courage and praised her work in aviation as a way of "breaking down the competitive struggle for social advantage between men and women."

The room erupted with applause as Amelia walked to the microphone. She shook Mrs. Meredith's hand and waved to the crowd. When the clapping stopped, she began by thanking Mrs. Meredith for her kind introduction. She also thanked President Elliott for inviting her to Purdue.

"Professors, staff, students, ladies and gentlemen, it is my great privilege to speak to you on this special occasion," she began.

Amelia described her adventures in aviation, including her flights across the Atlantic and Pacific Oceans. She encouraged women to strive to attain their goals, even if some called them "outside of their sphere."

I nudged Matt and whispered, "Non-traditional roles for women." He smiled and nodded.

In answer to the question, "Why do you fly?" Amelia said aviation had been her foremost ambition and that every oceanic flight contributed to the development of air transportation.

In closing, she said she hoped the public would overcome their fear of air travel. She stressed that airplanes were as safe as other modes of transportation. The audience applauded for a long time while Amelia smiled and waved.

"I had no idea she was such a good public speaker," Matt said.

"She does it a lot," I replied. "Over a hundred presentations a year." As we walked up the centre aisle to the outside door, I kept searching for Mabel.

The crowd lingered outside in the crisp autumn evening. Our group had trouble moving around them so we overheard a lot of comments.

"I think she should stick to flying," one man said. "How does she know what ordinary women want to do?"

"I think her husband is a saint," a woman replied. "He'd probably like her at home with a few children."

Matt leaned close to my ear. "It's just like being at Cary East."

"Let's keep walking," I whispered, "with our ears open."

Matt took my hand and the others followed in a line behind us.

A woman in a dark coat and hat spoke loudly. "The faculty wives support their husbands on this so-called 'women's issue.'"

"Speak for yourself, Edith," a woman in a wheelchair replied. "I would have jumped at the chance to go to university."

The first faculty wife rolled her eyes. "And how would you have done that, Clara?"

"That's the point. I didn't!"

Our line snaked its way to the sidewalk where we regrouped under the glow of a streetlight.

"Well, that was an interesting experience!" Matt said.

"Even Amelia Earhart can't please everyone," Jamie replied.

"She's still tops in my book," Ed said. "But I have to scram—big test tomorrow."

"I should get home, too," Jack said.

Jamie agreed and that left two of us to walk home together.

"You're awfully quiet," Matt said.

"Just thinking," I replied.

"Don't let those people upset you," he said. "Amelia knows what she's doing."

"In my mind I know that. But in my heart, I just want everyone to support her. She's worked hard and accomplished so much."

"Amelia knows it will take time."

"She told me that when she was in Harbour Grace. In fact, you sound just like her."

"I want to be a pilot but, unlike you and Amelia, I don't have to worry about changing the way people think," Matt said. "I know that sounds unfair but for now it's the way the world works."

I stopped and looked at him. "Now this is getting weird. That's *exactly* what Amelia said: 'Flying is easy; changing the way people think is hard.'"

"I guess we're both geniuses," he quipped.

I laughed. "I guess you are."

The night was clear and the stars shone brightly. The smell of burning leaves lingered in the air. I turned up my coat collar while we talked about the upcoming football game. Matt tried to explain the basics but since I'd never seen football, there was a lot of confusion and more laughter.

At the front steps of the residence, Matt cleared his throat before he spoke. "It's probably not the best time to mention this, with everything that's going on with Mabel, but...ah, would you like to go to the football game with me next Saturday?"

I considered it for a moment. "If I can patch things up with Mabel, could she come too?"

"Ah...sure," Matt replied. "We'll all go together."

"I'd like that."

We said good night and I waved as Matt walked away.

I went inside and up the stairs. Outside our door, I stopped and wondered what I could say to make up with Mabel.

The exact words wouldn't come to me, so I decided to play it by ear. The room was dark when I opened the door. I closed it behind me and paused.

"Are you awake?" I whispered.

Silence was the answer.

CHAPTER 13

CHOICES

———◄○►———

F IVE DAYS LATER, everyone was talking about the next big event at Purdue. The university was hosting a three-day conference on aeronautics under the supervision of the Mechanical Engineering School. Among the scheduled speakers were Amelia; Dean Potter, Dean of Engineering; Cap Aretz, Airport Manager; representatives of the Army Air Corps; and representatives of the aviation industry. Amelia was to speak at one thirty. Her topic was "Some Problems of Flight."

"What subject do you have this afternoon?" I asked Matt. We were standing on the front steps of the residence, waiting to go to our afternoon classes.

"Physics."

"Could you skip it?"

"You mean play hooky?" His eyes twinkled.

I grinned. "You could hear Amelia."

"What class do you have?" he asked.

"Don't worry, it's not Professor Jones's class. It's English with Professor Weeks, but he won't mind."

Matt stood up and, with a smile, pulled me off the steps.

At one-thirty we crept into room 254 of the Electrical Engineering Building. By sitting at the very back, we could slip in and out without being seen. Amelia spoke about the problems on her transoceanic flights.

Just before she ended her speech, I tugged Matt's sleeve and pointed to the door. If we made a quick escape, no one would know we had been there. We crouched down and hurried out...right into Professor Jones, who was going in to see the next speaker. He stepped back in surprise.

"Miss Ross?"

"Yes, sir." Matt and I stood up.

Professor Jones narrowed his eyes. "Matt Baker?"

"Yes, sir."

"I can hardly believe my eyes. *She* is nothing but trouble. But you? You're one of my best students." Professor Jones shook his head. "This is what happens when you let females into engineering."

Matt eased over in front of me and Professor Jones waved a finger in his face.

"Shape up, Mr. Baker—before it's too late!"

He stepped around Matt and opened the door. The sound of clapping became louder. Apparently Amelia had just finished speaking.

We continued walking when the door to the ladies' washroom opened at the end of the hall. Mabel hurried out and disappeared around the corner.

"Do you think she heard what her uncle said?" Matt asked.

"It might help me if she did," I replied. "She'd see the side of her uncle that we know."

It had been so hard sharing a room with someone who wouldn't talk to me. Especially when that someone had previously been so kind and helpful. I got a tight feeling in my chest when I thought about how much I missed my friend. My life felt like a jigsaw puzzle, with a missing piece in the middle.

Matt and I walked back to the residence in a sombre mood, knowing that I would pay for my decision to skip class. We said goodbye at the front steps of the Women's Residence and I walked up to my empty room.

The payment started the next day.

As soon as Professor Jones entered, he began his rant. "It seems *someone* doesn't value the opportunity she's being given here. She thinks she's so smart that she doesn't have to go to class." His voice got louder with each sentence. "Get up here, Mr. Baker, before she leads you astray too," he shouted.

I clutched Amelia's four-leaf clover in my pocket to give me strength. He was so angry and I didn't know what to expect.

Jamie collected his books and sat next to Jack in the front row. I was all alone in the back of the class. No one sat on either side or behind me. The boy in front of me was a whole row away. I was relieved that Professor Jones's rant didn't last longer, but nervous about what it might mean. Was he working on another plan to get me out of here? I'd been able to manage up until now, but who knew what else he had in store for me.

I closed my eyes and pictured myself getting off the train in Harbour Grace. There wasn't a soul to meet me because they all thought I'd be away for four years. I had to walk into the store and tell Mom and Nana that I wasn't going back to Purdue. I shook my head when I imagined them with no money for heat and light.

I opened my eyes. Failing was simply not an option.

—◦—

The class dragged on but ended without any more incidents. We all filed out, and I waited for the boys on the sidewalk.

"I'm sorry I didn't stand up for you," Jack said. "But I'm on a scholarship. I can't afford to get on the wrong side of Professor Jones."

"What did you do?" Jamie asked me.

I explained what had happened the previous afternoon. Both boys thought it had been a bad idea, even if it wasn't Professor Jones's class I'd skipped. Jamie reminded me that I was on a scholarship, too. I couldn't afford to get on the wrong side of any professor.

"Professor Jones would be against me no matter what I did," I pointed out.

"So, don't add fuel to his fire," Jamie advised. "I don't know what was in Matt's head! He should have known better." We walked in silence to the Women's Residence where the boys dropped me off.

After lunch, Matt was waiting for me outside the residence. When he saw me, he smiled and held out something wrapped in a hanky. "My mom's famous oatmeal raisin cookie will make you feel better."

"You heard what happened in class?"

He nodded. "Jamie told me. I'm sorry I didn't try to discourage you. I promise to do a better job the next time you get a crazy idea."

"Good. I need all the help I can get."

It felt good to have Matt on my side. Even more than Mabel, Jamie, and Jack, he knew what Professor Jones was capable of. I looked up at him and smiled.

He tucked my books under his arm and we headed to class.

———◦———

For the next two weeks, the conferences on "vocational plans" for female Purdue students continued. Finally, it was our turn to meet Amelia in small groups. I walked to the Memorial Union Building before five o'clock. The room had sofas, easy chairs, and a grand piano. After she shook hands with each girl, Amelia sat down and invited us to sit where she could see us. Mabel ran in at the last minute and the only chair left was next to me. When she sat down, she angled her body so that she didn't have to look at me. I could almost feel a chill coming off her. I sighed and wondered if this stalemate would ever end.

Just as she had done with the female professors at President Elliott's dinner, Amelia began by encouraging us to think outside the box. Since most of the girls were in home economics, she had many career possibilities for them to consider after graduation—health care, teaching, personnel work, management, industrial relations, social services, and writing. The hour passed quickly.

We rushed back to the residence, gulped down our dinner, and returned to the Union Building at seven o'clock for the large group session. We sat in the same seats as we had in the earlier session. I smiled at Mabel but she didn't smile back.

Amelia hopped up on the closed lid of the piano and asked us what we liked to do.

Mabel raised her hand first. "I like to work with my grandma at her boarding house."

"What do you do at your grandma's, Mabel?"

"I help her make up the weekly menus based on what's available or on sale; balance her budget based on what the boys pay for room and board; shop for groceries; and prepare the meals."

Amelia nodded and thought for a few seconds. "Let me ask for your career ideas first, Mabel."

"I don't have any."

"I'm going to put together all the things you like to do at your grandma's and see what I can come up with. Give me one minute." Amelia sat quietly and swung her legs while she thought. Everyone else sat quietly, too.

"See if you like this, Mabel," Amelia said. "You could manage the kitchen in a large institution such as a hospital, university, or military base. Some large businesses have their own kitchens and dining rooms for employees. Many of the jobs you're doing with your grandma would be required in management. You may also be required to hire staff and do other personnel work."

Mabel beamed. "I'd love that!" She opened her notebook and started writing.

I looked at Mabel's big smile and wished I could make her as happy as she was at this moment.

By the end of the discussion, Elizabeth wanted to write for a magazine or have her own newspaper column, Joan planned to be a clothes designer, Barb leaned toward social service, and Faye wanted to work in the health field. "Maybe as a food inspector," she said.

"As you can see, there are possibilities in many fields," Amelia said. "Ginny wants to be a pilot, and she'll be a good one, but you need to find your own dream and hang onto it."

"What if...I just want to be a wife and mother?" Sarah asked hesitantly.

"That's fine," Amelia replied. "Just don't settle for something because you don't know what the possibilities are."

"My mom works from home," Elizabeth said. "She takes care of the account books for Dr. O'Toole, the local vet. She gets a little money and free medical care for our farm animals."

"Oh!" Mabel's hand shot into the air. "My mom gives music lessons. People pay her with vegetables, eggs, butter, milk, and sewing."

Amelia held out her hands and others talked about what their mothers did from home. I didn't raise my hand because

Amelia had been to Harbour Grace. She already knew that Mom sewed for the rich ladies in St. John's and Nana bartered her knitting for any supplies we needed, much like Mabel's mom.

Before we left, Amelia asked us to fill out a questionnaire she'd written. She asked us to indicate the year we were in, our age, whether we had ever worked, and whether we were working while attending Purdue. The rest of the questions were related to whether we would seek employment after finishing university.

Every girl handed in a questionnaire—even Sarah, who now had permission to be whatever she wanted.

CHAPTER 14

CHANGE

————◄○►————

THERE WAS ANOTHER note on the door when I got home. I hurried into our room to find Mabel sitting at her desk. I decided to share it with her since it wasn't about Uncle Malcolm.

"This is from Amelia." I sat at my desk, tore open the envelope and started to read aloud:

> *Dear Ginny,*
>
> *I'm afraid this is goodbye. As you know, I was supposed to be here for another week. But an opportunity has come up that I can't refuse. All my formal presentations have been completed, except the Conference on Women's Work Opportunities on Friday. Dean Fisher is giving a blanket excuse to all students who want to attend a session. There will be no penalty for missed classes. You will be told about this first thing tomorrow morning.*

You're invited to join me for lunch at President Elliott's house on Friday. Then we can all go to my last presentation together.

Give my best to Mabel. If lunch was at my house, she'd be there. But I can't impose another guest on my hostess. We can meet her at the Electrical Engineering Building at 1:30 P.M. I'll leave directly from there.

Affectionately, A

I felt like I'd been punched in the stomach. All my worrying about Mabel and now Amelia was leaving. I walked to my bed and sat down.

"I'm not ready for this," I said aloud.

Mabel stood up, paused, and slowly crossed the room. She sat beside me for a few seconds before she reached for my hand and patted it. "Nobody likes a sudden change," she said.

I wasn't sure if the "nobody" was referring to her or me, but I didn't want to spoil the moment by asking questions. We were sitting together and talking and that was all that mattered.

"You'll get to have lunch with Amelia and meet Ed's parents," Mabel said.

I nodded and squeezed her hand.

Over the next few hours, life seemed to get back to normal. Mabel remained quieter than her usual bubbly self but we went down to dinner together. For the first time in ages, my stomach didn't turn over at the sight of food.

When we returned to our room, we did our homework and crawled into bed. I curled up but couldn't fall asleep. I kept thinking about what Mabel had said. She was right; I didn't like the sudden change in Amelia's plans. I still had so many questions to ask her.

But did Mabel mean that she was experiencing a sudden change too? Did she hear what her uncle said after Amelia's presentation? Did she finally realize what he was really like? Had she changed her opinion about him? And was this the sudden change she didn't like? Then I remembered something Amelia had said about her transatlantic flight. Even though she had gasoline dripping down her neck and flames outside the windshield, she had to carry on. There was nothing she could do to change the situation.

That was when I realized the answers to my questions didn't matter. I needed to pass Professor Jones's class or I would fail first-year engineering. Mabel needed Uncle Malcolm to pay her tuition. Like Amelia, there was nothing we could do to change our situations.

———◇———

The next morning at breakfast, Mabel chatted with everyone. The sparkle had returned to her eyes, and they lit up even more when Miss Schleman announced Dean Fisher's blanket excuse for the Conference on Women's Work Opportunities. The girls cheered and checked the schedule for the session they wanted to attend. Most chose Amelia's. I tried to be excited about it but I wasn't having much success.

I walked to class with a heavy heart, Mabel beside me.

"I'll help you choose an outfit for the president's lunch," she offered.

I knew Mabel was trying to cheer me up. "Thanks," I said. "Instead of missing Amelia, I should be happy she was here. She gave us as much time as she could."

"That's right!" Mabel shifted her books and put her arm around my elbow.

"Thanks," I said.

"What for?"

"Being my friend again."

Mabel squeezed my elbow. "Ditto."

After class, we met back at the residence and walked into the foyer together. Miss Schleman stood near her office with an envelope in her hand. She called us over and handed it to me.

"It's from Amelia," I whispered to Mabel.

Miss Schleman smiled. "Off you go and read it in private."

We thanked her and ran up to our room. I sat on my bed and Mabel plopped down beside me.

Dear Ginny,

After dinner with the Elliotts, I have a final meeting about my return to Purdue next fall. I should be back around 9:30 P.M. I've had an open-door policy with the seniors in the guest wing so they could drop in and chat whenever I was there. When I get home, I'll slip in and leave the door closed. That way we can have a short visit before I go. Bring Mabel.

Affectionately, A

I turned to Mabel. "Want to go?"

Mabel stood up and casually walked to her desk. She opened a book and said, "I think I'm free."

We laughed until we had tears in our eyes.

At 9:25, we left our room, walked downstairs, and looked both ways before we slipped into the living room. A senior opened the door from the hallway where Amelia's room was located and shouted to others to hurry up.

Mabel and I plopped down on the nearest sofa and grabbed magazines off the coffee table. Three girls walked toward us. We looked up and smiled. As soon as the room was clear, we entered the guest wing and I tapped lightly on the door to room 101. When it swung open, Amelia took my hand and pulled me inside. Mabel followed and gently closed the door.

"I'm so sorry we haven't had a chance to properly visit until now," Amelia said. "Sit down so we can catch up."

I walked to the sofa and Amelia sat beside me. She held her hand out to indicate a chair for Mabel. For the next few minutes I told Amelia that nothing much had changed in Harbour Grace. Billy had taken over my job at the hotel, Mom was still selling her sewing to the few women in St. John's who still had money to buy it, and Nana was the best barterer in town.

"Was Harbour Grace the second time you met?" Mabel asked.

"It was," Amelia replied. "Has Ginny told you how we first met?"

"Only that she ran away from home to find you and you gave her a lucky four-leaf clover."

"Let me fill in the details that even Ginny doesn't know. She arrived in the pouring rain and a sorrier sight you'll never see. To make matters worse, she dropped to her knees in the mud when I came to the door. My housekeeper, Mrs. Waddell, gave her a bath, some dry clothes, and something to eat. Then Ginny joined my husband, George, our friend, Bernt Balchen, and me in the living room."

"I remember that!" I said with a smile.

"Here's the part you don't know. The three of us had been planning my transatlantic flight from Harbour Grace, Newfoundland, when you walked in."

"I remember your friend rolling up a map as soon as he saw me."

"Do you remember the first thing you said to us?" Amelia asked.

I shook my head. "I only remember feeling completely overwhelmed."

"You said, 'I'm Ginny Ross from Harbour Grace, Newfoundland.'" Amelia reached for my hand. "I felt as if a good omen had just walked into my life. After Mrs. Waddell took you to bed, I told George and Bernt that you were a sign of our success. They just laughed at me but I don't believe in coincidences."

"Are you saying Ginny is your good luck charm?" Mabel asked.

Amelia smiled. "I have to admit I'm superstitious, but that's not the reason I suggested Ginny apply to Purdue."

Amelia stood up, crossed her arms over her chest, and paced in front of us while she spoke. "I remember sitting in Aunt Rose's kitchen when Uncle Harry walked in and confirmed Ginny's observations. The tire on my plane had been damaged. He told me what Ginny could do with engines...and I saw the same longing in her eyes that I had as a twelve-year-old. I knew then I would support her in any way I could."

"I don't hear that a lot around here," I murmured.

"Most people think engineers and pilots should be men," Amelia said.

I nodded but avoided looking at Mabel. We'd been working hard not to mention Uncle Malcolm or Professor Jones.

Amelia sat down beside me again. "If you're going to be a trailblazer, you have to get used to people who think differently from you."

"I'll never get used to them."

"You already have. You're here."

"But this is different from Harbour Grace—and you helped me get here."

Amelia shook her head. "I only mentioned to President Elliott that I knew a promising young female pilot. He said he hoped you'd apply."

"That's it?"

"You had to have the marks and the ability to explain why you chose this university."

"Really?" I asked.

"If I didn't think you were capable of becoming a pilot, I wouldn't have encouraged you." She reached for my hands. "You've got what it takes, Ginny Ross from Harbour Grace, Newfoundland—never forget that." She stood up and pulled me into a big hug. "On that note, I'll send you off to bed while I get ready for my presentation tomorrow."

She turned and shook Mabel's hand, before the three of us walked to the door and said goodnight. The door closed quietly behind us and we retraced our steps back through the living room.

"I can't believe what just happened," Mabel said. "I just sat and talked with Amelia Earhart! Did you know you were her lucky charm?"

I laughed. "I wouldn't go that far...but it adds to the story I already knew."

I held out my elbow and we walked upstairs arm in arm. Mabel chatted on about Amelia and I realized I'd learned a lot myself tonight. Amelia hadn't arranged my acceptance to Purdue after all. She believed I belonged here. She believed I could succeed.

When we got to our room I sat down at my desk and took Mom's hanky out of my pocket. I held it up to my nose and breathed in the smell of lavender.

"I will make you proud," I whispered. "All of you."

CHAPTER 15

GOODBYE

———◆———

T HE NEXT DAY was Friday and I felt like I was on a roller
coaster. One minute I was excited about seeing Amelia,
but the next I was terrified that she was leaving. Mabel and I
met back in our room after our first class. Amelia was speaking
at two o'clock, so I had to get to the Elliotts for lunch as soon
as I could.

"What about my green velvet dress?"

"Too dressy," Mabel replied. She walked from my closet to
her own, draping clothes over her arm. "Your navy skirt with
my white blouse and Black Watch jacket."

"Your what jacket?"

"It's a navy and dark green tartan." Mabel laid each piece on
my bed. "And my silk stockings, not socks, with your shoes."

"Yes, boss!"

I put everything on and looked at myself in the mirror over
my dresser. Mabel had good fashion sense. The whole outfit
looked great. I felt smart and sophisticated—and only had

to scrub my hands three times to remove the engine grease embedded under my nails.

I repeated Mabel's directions to the Elliotts' house out loud and hurried down the stairs. At the front door, I waved and Mabel waved back.

"See you at one thirty," she called.

My sadness about Amelia's departure was easing and excitement about the lunch was increasing.

The Elliotts' large stone house was easy to find. I walked up the front steps and rang the brass bell. Ed opened the door with a big smile. "Come on in. I'll introduce you to my mom and dad."

I had already seen President Elliott at various events but never met him. "So, you're Ginny Ross from Harbour Grace, Newfoundland," he said. "I've heard a lot about you from Amelia and Ed."

I smiled and shook his outstretched hand. "How do you do, sir?"

"This is my mother," Ed said. A tall, elegant woman in a dark green dress stepped forward.

"Thank you for inviting me to lunch," I said as I shook her hand.

"And, of course, you already know Amelia," President Elliott said.

She gave me a hug. "Good to see you," she whispered in my ear.

"We don't have much time for lunch," Mrs. Elliott said. "I think we'll go straight into the dining room." She held out her hand to Amelia, who walked in first; I was next, followed by President Elliott, and Ed. Mrs. Elliott came in last but everyone stood behind his or her chair until she sat down.

All those table manners Nana and Mom drilled into me now made sense. I knew when to put my napkin on my lap, what cutlery to use, and how to sit between courses—hands in my lap, with good posture.

Most of the conversation was between Amelia and President Elliott about her future plans at Purdue. He drew me into the conversation during the roast chicken course. "Cap Aretz tells me he took you up in a Taylor Cub."

"It was my first time in the air and it was amazing."

"Ginny will make an excellent pilot," Amelia said.

I smiled and looked at my lap. I was slightly embarrassed by the praise, but I got that warm feeling again.

"Matt Baker said she knows more about planes than any girl he's ever met," Ed added.

"I trust anything Matt Baker says," President Elliott replied. "Cap says Matt is his best student."

"Are you happy at Purdue, Ginny?" Mrs. Elliott asked.

I glanced at Ed and answered, "Yes."

"What would you change if you could?" she pressed.

I thought about Professor Jones. His absence would make a positive change for female engineering students, but I wasn't prepared to bring that up. I didn't want to act like a tattletale. "I wish there were more girls in my classes," I said instead.

"All of us around this table share that wish," President Elliott said.

"You're working on it and that's the important thing," said Amelia.

As soon as we finished dessert, Mrs. Elliott stood up and announced it was time to leave. We climbed into President Elliott's car to get to the Electrical Engineering Building. He pulled into a special parking spot with his name on it. He and Amelia went to the back door and the rest of us walked to the front door to meet Mabel.

"Mother, this is a friend of ours, Mabel Anderson," Ed said. "Amelia suggested she meet us here."

Mrs. Elliott held out her hand. "How do you do, Mabel?"

"Fine, thank you." she replied.

A student usher led us to our seats in the front row. Mrs. Elliott continued her conversation with Mabel as we sat down. I heard her ask Mabel if she was happy at Purdue. When Mabel said she loved it, I knew what the next question would be.

I leaned over slightly and heard, "What would you change here, if you could?"

Mabel hesitated for a few seconds. "I'd like to see more girls in all the programs...and I'd like them to be more accepted, like we are in home economics."

"Girls aren't accepted in the other courses?"

"Some of the boys—and even some of the professors—aren't very welcoming."

Mrs. Elliott raised her eyebrows. "Then we must do more to correct that."

Before Mabel could answer, President Elliott walked onto the stage and the audience applauded. He smiled and waited for silence. He introduced Amelia and the crowd clapped louder.

She spoke about the new Lockheed Electra 10E that the Purdue Research Foundation had purchased for her, and how she would use it for various projects. The rest of the time it would remain at the Purdue University Airport. Then she described the type of research for which the plane could be used.

But I wasn't listening. My mind was in Rye, New York, where I first met Amelia; in Harbour Grace, where we met in Aunt Rose's kitchen; and here at Purdue in the Women's Residence. On stage stood the public Amelia but I thought about the private Amelia—her laugh, the space between her front teeth, and her tight hugs.

The crowd clapped again and Amelia smiled and waved. Mrs. Elliott, Mabel, Ed, and I walked through a door to the back of the stage. President Elliott led us back to the car, where Mrs. Elliott pulled the others to one side to give Amelia and me a few minutes alone.

She hugged me tightly. "Remember, you can do this."

"I wish I was as sure as you are." The lump in my throat was growing. "Sometimes I get so scared...."

"I do too." Amelia stepped back. She held onto my shoulders and looked directly into my eyes. "I wish I had all the answers for you, Ginny, but I don't. Each of us has to find her own path and stick to it no matter what. I'm doing the best I can but it's not easy. There are a lot of people who think I'm a pushy woman who doesn't know where she belongs."

I smiled when I thought of the comments I'd heard after Convocation. "If *you're* being criticized what chance do I have?"

"The same as any of us who step outside our accepted roles." Amelia squeezed my hands. "You have to expect criticism if you choose a non-traditional job. It's part of the process of change."

"Learning to fly is easy," I replied. "Changing the way people think is hard."

"You remembered!" Amelia smiled and hugged me again.

Then she turned, shook hands with all the others, and thanked them. "Take care of our friend," she whispered to Mabel.

President Elliott opened the car door for Amelia and walked around to the driver's side. He kissed Mrs. Elliott's cheek and shook Ed's hand. "I'll see you in three days," he said.

My stomach lurched when the car started up. As it pulled away, my heart pounded and I couldn't catch my breath. Every cell in my body ached to run after it.

I wiped away my tears before I turned to the others. Mrs. Elliott patted my hand but no one spoke. We walked under the tall oaks along the sidewalk. At the corner of State and Russell Streets, I turned to Mrs. Elliott and thanked her for her hospitality and kindness.

"It was a pleasure meeting you and Mabel," she said. "I hope Ed will bring you to see me again."

We all shook hands and headed in opposite directions. Mabel put her arm around my shoulders.

"It won't be long until Amelia makes her next historic flight. And she'll make sure you're a part of it."

CHAPTER 16

PROMISE

————◀◉▶————

AMELIA'S LEAVING CHANGED everything. At least, that's how it seemed to me. The daylight faded sooner, strong winds blew the remaining leaves from the trees, and an icy cold gripped the campus. I wore my winter coat, wool hat, and mittens. My sealskin boots stood in the closet, waiting for the snow.

The next class with Professor Jones added to the gloom. He strode in and slammed his books on the counter at the front. "Who skipped class to go to the Conference on Women's Work Opportunities?"

Although the answer was obvious, I raised my hand. Before I lowered it, he was marching down the aisle toward me. A chair scraped across the floor. Without turning around, Professor Jones shouted over his shoulder, "Sit *down*, Mr. Stinson or you'll be judged by the company you keep."

Every boy in the class turned to face me. Many smiled in anticipation.

Professor Jones stopped in front of my desk and crossed his arms. "Why are you here?"

"Dean Fisher gave us a blanket excuse to go to the conference."

"You didn't answer my question, Miss Ross. *Why* are you *here?*"

"I want to be a pilot."

"Well, my dear, if you want to become a pilot, you have to attend classes." He stared down at me and continued. "Since you are not willing to do that, you had better leave." He stepped back and gestured toward the door.

My heart raced but I knew better than to move. I sat and thought about what Amelia had said. "Find your own path and stick to it no matter what." If that was good enough for Amelia, it was good enough for me. I repeated the sentence to myself until Professor Jones turned abruptly and walked up the aisle.

Over his shoulder, he said, "See me after class, Miss Ross."

My hands shook as I opened my book and started copying notes from the blackboard. I didn't hear much of the lecture because I kept reminding myself of what Ed had said. "If you write a good exam, Professor Jones will have to give you a good mark."

Shuffling noises made me look up. The class was over and the boys were closing their books. A few of them spoke to Professor Jones on their way out. I lowered my head and walked to the front of the class, dreading what was coming. When the room was empty, Professor Jones told me to sit down and then he closed the door.

"So, you want to be a pilot," he said.

"Yes, sir." I kept my eyes on the desk.

"Like Miss 'La Dee Da' Earhart."

"Yes, sir."

"Every boy in here needs an education to support a wife and family." Professor Jones opened his arms to indicate the empty classroom. "And you're here to make a name for yourself."

"That's not true."

"You'll get married, have children, and stop dabbling in aviation. Then some poor chump will have to support you."

The lump in my throat was growing. *I need to support a family too*, I thought to myself. I looked up and said quietly, "You don't know me."

"I don't have to know you," he shouted. "I know your kind— sitting with the president's wife and son in the front row, leaving with them from backstage, riding on Amelia Earhart's coattails. You're a liar and a fraud."

I jumped to my feet and stared into Professor Jones's face. His forehead shone with moisture. Spit had dried in the corners of his mouth. My heart pounded so hard I was afraid he would hear it.

I wanted to scream "I'm no fraud!" I wanted to throw my books and cry and yell that he had no idea what I'd sacrificed to be here. But I knew losing my temper would only work to his advantage. He wanted to see me hysterical and out of control so he could say I was just an overly emotional woman who didn't deserve to be here.

"Go on," he goaded. "Stomp out of here like the rest of your kind."

Find your own path and stick to it no matter what, I repeated to myself. The pounding in my chest slowed and I sat down.

He bent over and whispered into my face. "I'll see you out of here."

I kept my eyes lowered.

"You can't win this battle, Miss Ross."

I heard him walk behind the counter and clear his throat. I looked up to see him wiping the corners of his mouth and loosening his tie. He stood for a few seconds before telling me to get out.

I scrambled to my feet and got halfway to the door before I heard my name. I turned to find him pointing his finger at me. "You're gone," he whispered.

Outside the door, I ran into Jack and Jamie. We hurried out to the front steps and down to the sidewalk.

"Are you okay?" Jack asked. "I was so afraid you'd leave when he pointed to the door."

"Not me," Jamie replied. "I knew you wouldn't move."

"What did he say?" Jack asked. "We could only hear a few words through the closed door."

"He said a lot of things but the message was clear: I'm a fraud. I don't belong here and he's going to make sure I leave."

Jamie nodded. "I can't wait to tell Matt and Ed. Good old Professor Jones has met his match."

I didn't answer. I was still shaking from the experience. Instead of embarrassing me in front of the entire class, Professor Jones had threatened me in private. Somehow that had been more frightening, in a way I couldn't explain.

The boys kept up the conversation as we headed toward the Women's Residence. They discussed our next class with Professor Jones, the upcoming football game, and exams. I wondered if I should tell Mabel what had happened in class. I didn't want to upset her by bringing up Uncle Malcolm, but keeping secrets hadn't worked either. When we approached the front steps, Mabel walked down to meet us.

"This is my roommate, Mabel Anderson."

The boys shook her hand and told her their names. "You should have seen Ginny today!" Jamie said.

"Why?" Mabel asked.

"Professor Jones told her to leave the class but she refused," Jack replied proudly.

Mabel turned to me. "He didn't accept the blanket excuse from Dean Fisher?"

"He called me a fraud and said he'd see me out of there."

Mabel put her hand over her mouth.

"Don't worry," I said, squaring my shoulders. "I'm going to write an amazing exam. If I get a good mark, he'll have to pass me! That's what Ed said, and he should know."

CHAPTER 17

FOOTBALL

—◄○►—

I HADN'T SLEPT well. Every time I closed my eyes, Professor Jones's face appeared, leaning over me and saying, "You can't win this battle, Miss Ross." I rolled over to find Mabel in front of her mirror, dabbing lipstick onto her cheek and rubbing it in.

"Football day, roomie!" she announced.

Once Mabel and I were friends again, I told her that Matt had offered to take both of us to the game. Since her brothers had played in high school, she had been much more excited by the prospect than I had been. She understood how the game was actually played.

I stood up and stretched. At least I wouldn't have to see Professor Jones today. There was only one class in the morning so everyone could go to the game. I would be seeing Professor Abernathy, which meant it would be a good day.

The morning flew by and as soon as lunch was over, most of the girls went upstairs to get ready. Miss Schleman stopped

Mabel and me as we walked out of the dining room. There are two gentlemen waiting for you in date room number one."

We thanked her and she walked back down the hall to her office.

"Who are the two gentlemen?" Mabel asked.

I shrugged. "Matt and someone else, I expect."

The four "date rooms" stood to the left of the main living room. They were small sitting rooms with no doors. That way a girl was never really alone with a boy. Everyone who walked by looked in and some even stopped to talk.

Mabel and I found the Baker boys side by side on the sofa. Jamie looked uncomfortable but Matt must have done this before. He stood up calmly when we walked in. Jamie looked at his brother and jumped to his feet.

Mabel smiled and said, "Look what Ginny made."

"A list of players!" I held it out to the boys.

Matt chuckled. "For someone who has never seen football, that will definitely help."

It was a sunny but cool day as we walked to Ross Ade Stadium. I had never seen so many people in one place at one time. Rows of them sat around a green, oval field, with white lines and numbers on it. Two, large upright poles joined by a crossbar stood at each end. Matt led us to a section of seats that overlooked the middle of the field. We walked ten rows up the centre aisle before we sat down. I could see both ends of the field without turning my head, so I assumed they must be good seats.

"Okay. Here's all you need to know," Matt said. "Purdue will be wearing black and gold. Iowa will be in green and white. Both teams want to move the ball in the direction they're facing. When they get the ball into the end zone, they get points."

"Right," I said.

The game progressed just as Matt said. Even though I didn't understand the specifics, I joined the crowd and yelled each time Purdue moved the ball in the right direction. The game ended with Purdue winning 38 to 24.

As we left the stadium, Mabel and I waved to Elizabeth, Joanne, and Barb, but Matt told us we'd have to hurry if we wanted to get seats at the coffee shop.

We managed to get the last table and Matt ordered for all of us. While we drank our root beer, we talked about the game. They couldn't believe I'd never eaten a hot dog, shelled peanuts, or seen a marching band.

"I bet you've never eaten fish and brewis, jigged for cod, or seen a seal."

They all laughed but I had made my point. It was a long way from Newfoundland to West Lafayette.

While we walked home, the other three continued to discuss the game but my mind was still in Harbour Grace. I smelled the salt cod drying on the flakes and felt the paralyzing cold when I waded along the rocky shore, looking for shells. What I missed the most was the hiss of salt water as the waves flowed back over the pebbles to the sea.

Matt turned to me and asked if I was all right. I described what I'd been picturing in my mind. He took hold of my hand and gave it a squeeze. "It must be hard to be so far from home." I smiled up at him and nodded.

We paused at the front steps of the Women's Residence and Mabel thanked Jamie for the wonderful afternoon. I said the same to Matt.

"Could the four of us do this again?" Matt asked.

"Sure!" Mabel replied.

I smiled, but couldn't help thinking about Llew. While I was socializing with new friends, he was all alone on a coastal steamer. I felt like I was being unfaithful to someone I loved.

CHAPTER 18

GOOD NEWS

——◄o►——

O UR END-OF-SEMESTER EXAMS began on a cold, blustery
Wednesday. Lead-coloured clouds rolled across the sky.
Wet snow clung to tree branches and I wore my sealskin boots
for the first time since arriving in Indiana.

Most students were nervous about the exams, but not me.
This was my chance to prove to Professor Jones that I belonged
in his class. Mabel, Matt, Jamie, Jack, and I had studied hard,
mostly in the library. We made up a schedule and took breaks
at the same time. Then we walked to the Union Building for
coffee, hot chocolate, or tea. The boys walked us back to the
Women's Residence when we were too tired to study any more.

I wrote the English exam first and found it easy. By
predicting which questions would be asked and studying the
answers, I had been well prepared.

Professor Jones's practical exam was given at the Michael
Golden Shops on the last day of classes but the written exam
was the day after English. I worked even harder for that one.

Jamie, Jack, and I walked together to our regular classroom. Professor Jones stood behind the counter at the front and greeted the boys as they arrived. Jamie and Jack got a nod, but he didn't look at me. We took our usual seats, which meant it was quiet back where I was.

The exam was sitting face down on our desks, with a note on the blackboard telling us to wait for directions before turning it over. Some of the boys tried to read the questions through the back of the paper, but I was content to wait. I knew the work and I looked forward to proving it.

"Nine o'clock, gentlemen," Professor Jones announced. "You may begin."

I took a deep breath, turned over my paper, and scanned the whole exam before I started. I smiled at what I saw and then circled back to the first question:

1. Given the choice between a turbocharger and a supercharger, which would you choose for higher altitude flights? Justify your answer.

Let's see, I said to myself. *Both turbochargers and superchargers increase power and efficiency. So, the key must be the higher altitude. Both use air compressors to send oxygen-rich intake air to the engine, so why would one be preferable to the other? It must be what powers the compressor; a turbocharger uses hot engine exhaust while a supercharger uses a geared mechanism driven off the crankshaft. Altitude wouldn't affect a geared mechanism, but at higher altitudes the hot exhaust gases would expand more in the thinner air. So, the turbocharger would supply more power to the turbine!*

I scribbled my answer, fully explaining my thought process, and sat back to see Professor Jones staring at me from the front of the room. Was he trying to intimidate me? If so, it wouldn't work. The exam was just what I'd expected. I rubbed my hands together. On to question two.

———◄○►———

After the exam I walked back to the residence with Jamie. "How do you think you did?" he asked.

"I'll have a mark between 90 and 100 percent," I replied. "I knew all the answers but I'll deduct ten percent for the unexpected."

Jamie smiled. "I wish I was that confident!"

The following day, Professor Abernathy approached me. I had just written his exam and was leaving the Physics Building.

"How did you find my exam, Miss Ross?" he asked.

"Fine, thank you, sir."

"Will you be going home for Christmas?"

"I'm afraid not." Money was the reason, but I didn't want to bring that up with one of my professors.

Money, or more precisely the lack of it, was never far from my mind. I almost shivered at the thought of the wind rattling the windows facing the bay back home. In their letters, Mom and Nana always said they were fine but I knew that depended on whether Billy was still working to buy coal and electricity.

"Our housekeeper wants to visit her mother in Alabama and Mrs. Abernathy wondered if you might help us out," he continued.

"I'd love to!"

"We would pay you, of course."

"When can I start?"

"As soon as the exams end, Mildred will show you her routines before she leaves. If you like, we could advance your salary so you can buy presents before Christmas."

"That would be wonderful." I took hold of Professor Abernathy's hand and shook it vigorously. I wouldn't be buying presents but I would be sending money home.

He smiled and told me to come over at eight on December 12. I could work until January 5 when Mildred returned. I didn't even wait for Jamie. I ran all the way to the residence to tell Mabel the good news.

———◇———

The rest of the exams were a breeze. Still, I was glad they were over. Work started the next day. I walked to the address Professor Abernathy had given me. The cold air felt refreshing. Not as refreshing as the salt-sea air off the bay, but it still put a bounce in my step.

"I'se the b'y that builds the boats, and I'se the b'y that sails 'em," I sang quietly.

The Abernathys' house looked like many others on campus: two storeys, red brick, brass doorbell. I pushed the bell and listened to the muffled footsteps approaching the door from the other side. Professor Abernathy opened the door and invited me in. He hung up my hat and coat while I pulled off my sealskin boots and placed them on a mat next to the closet.

We walked into the living room together, where a woman with short white hair and bright blue eyes sat in a wheelchair.

"Ginny, this is my wife, Clara," Professor Abernathy said.

"Come in, my dear, and sit down." She held out her hand and I shook it.

"You were at Convocation," I said.

"How do you remember that?"

"I overheard you say you'd have jumped at the opportunity to attend university. I didn't think a wheelchair should have stopped you."

"How kind you are to say that."

"Clara loves to read," Professor Abernathy said. "Perhaps you could share some of the books you're reading in English class."

"I'd be happy to," I replied.

A tall woman with short blonde hair entered the room. Mrs. Abernathy turned to me and introduced Mildred, the woman I would be replacing for a few weeks.

"It will make me feel better if I know my people are in good hands," Mildred said. "Let's get started in the kitchen."

Mildred washed the dishes and I dried. I laid them on the kitchen table until we had finished. Then Mildred showed me where everything was kept. As well as keeping the kitchen clean and neat, I was responsible for grocery shopping and preparing all the meals.

Uncle Harry would laugh if he heard about the meals. I remember the first time I made soup at the hotel. He helped me understand the cooking terminology and then concluded by saying, "I think I'll have a sandwich for lunch." My cooking had improved with Aunt Rose's lessons, but I still wasn't up to his high standard of culinary skill.

Dry mopping the hardwood floors and dusting came next. The living room was empty while we worked. "We don't keep carpets on the floor because of Mrs. Abernathy's wheelchair," Mildred said.

When we'd finished, it was time to prepare lunch. We worked like a team. Mildred seasoned the soup, while I made egg salad sandwiches. We were putting the cutlery and glasses on a tray when Mrs. Abernathy came in.

"You can walk!" I cried. Then I immediately clapped my hand over my mouth.

Mrs. Abernathy and Mildred laughed.

"You must be confused," Mrs. Abernathy said. "Sit down and I'll explain. I had rheumatic fever as a child and the disease damaged my heart. I have to take my time with everything I do. Too much exertion isn't good."

"What can you manage?" I asked.

"I do light housekeeping, like dusting, drying the dishes, and setting the table. I write letters, arrange flowers, knit, sew, or read for the rest of the morning. In the afternoon, I lie down and rest."

"When do you use your wheelchair?"

"I only use it in the house when I'm tired. Charles and I were at a Christmas party last night. That's why I was using it earlier. I always use it when I go out. Walking long distances or up and down stairs is very difficult. That's why our bedroom is on the ground floor."

I nodded. "What do you like to do for fun?"

"My first love is reading. In the evenings, Charles and I play cards or listen to the radio. He put up a special antenna so we can pull in stations from quite a distance."

"Sorry to interrupt," Mildred said, "but it's time for lunch." Mrs. Abernathy excused herself and went into the dining room.

I peeked out the kitchen door until Professor Abernathy arrived from the university five minutes later. He sat down at the dining room table and squeezed his wife's hand. "How was your morning, my dear?"

Mildred sent me in with the soup. I bumped open the kitchen door with my hip, the way I used to at Aunt Rose's hotel. Next, I brought in the sandwiches. I saw Mildred peeking into the dining room.

Back in the kitchen, Mildred gave me an approving nod. "You've done this before," she said. I told her about the Archibald Hotel in Harbour Grace and she nodded again. "I think you're just what the Abernathys need."

———⋖◦⋗———

A week later, Professor Abernathy wrestled a live evergreen tree through the front door, while Mrs. Abernathy clapped her hands with delight. He and I dragged it to the metal stand he'd placed in the corner, next to the fireplace. With a lot of pulling, grunting, and adjusting, we finally got it standing straight.

Professor Abernathy brought in the boxes of decorations and lights. We placed them on the tree, according to Mrs.

Abernathy's directions. She sat on the sofa and pointed to where everything should go. Her eyes shone as the Christmas tree came to life.

Indiana was red brick buildings, railway tracks, flat land, and cornfields. Home was rocks, bays, wind, and boats. But Christmas in both places was an evergreen tree, decorations, and presents, no matter how small. At this very moment, Nana was probably sitting on the sofa in our living room and pointing to where Mom and Billy should hang the decorations—and her eyes would be shining too.

"I think we'll have our Christmas dinner at five o'clock," Mrs. Abernathy said. "I love a crackling fire when it's dark outside and candles flickering on the table."

I smiled and nodded. "That's what we do back home too."

"Let's talk about the menu." She patted the sofa next to her and I sat down. We agreed on Virginia baked ham, mashed potatoes, carrots, turnips, and Brussels sprouts. I sighed quietly with relief. I was afraid they'd want turkey, dressing, and gravy. At home, Mom always made the dressing and Nana always made the gravy.

Before I left, Professor Abernathy brought in eggnog and turned out all the lights. Our silver cups reflected the flames from the fireplace and the decorations on the tree. In spite of being so far from Harbour Grace, I felt at home.

I took out Mom's hanky to wipe my nose but what I was really doing was breathing in the scent of lavender.

CHAPTER 19

CHRISTMAS

——◀○▶——

T HE FOLLOWING WEEK, Professor Jones sent out invitations to his Christmas dinner. I asked to read Jamie's because I didn't get one.

"Maybe yours got lost in the mail," Jack said. The three of us burst out laughing.

Jamie stated he wasn't going if I couldn't come. Jack agreed, but I insisted they go. They had to be my eyes and ears at the party.

"Professor Jones is a puzzle that I'd like to solve," I said.

Jamie looked at Jack, who shrugged. "All right, but only because you asked."

Jack, Jamie, and I were at the coffee shop waiting for Mabel and Matt. I had finished work at the Abernathys' and Jamie had finished at the dairy barns. He and Matt were filling in for the agriculture students who had gone home for Christmas. Mabel worked at the library but finished later than us.

She walked in and stomped the snow off her boots. After she hung up her coat and hat, she joined us. Jamie moved over to let her sit down.

"How are the Abernathys?" she asked.

"Kind and considerate. I love working there."

Before I could ask about the library, Mabel filled us in. "I love my job too. Because most of the students have gone home, the building is quiet and peaceful."

Jamie waved to Matt who stood at the door. He went through the same routine as Mabel before he sat down. The waitress came over and Matt ordered coffee and apple pie.

"Where are you working, Jack?" Matt asked once he was settled.

"Mostly at home—not making money but saving it." He sipped his coffee. "My parents get paid extra to work overtime at Christmas, so I keep my sisters on track."

"Doing what?" Jamie asked.

"Making sure they do their chores, cooking, and washing up."

Mabel looked at me. "A non-traditional role for men."

"Amelia would be proud of you, Jack," I said.

Jack smiled and challenged Jamie and Matt to describe what they did at home. The next half hour passed in teasing and laughing. Apparently, the Baker boys were not much help around the house.

"It's not our fault," Matt protested. "Our mother says we make her work twice as hard when we help out."

"On that flimsy excuse, I'll be going," Jack said. "Some of us begin work before Mommy serves us breakfast!"

I looked at Matt and shook my head. "Amelia would *not* be proud of you."

Jack laughed and stood up. "Time for me to get home."

We waved to him before he went out the door. The waitress came over and we ordered another round of coffee.

"Have you asked Mabel?" Matt looked at his brother.

Mabel sat up. "Asked me what?"

"Oh, uh, there's a New Year's Eve party at the Union Building," Jamie said, suddenly shy. A blush crept from his cheeks up to his blond hairline. "Would you like to go...with me?"

Mabel was radiant. "Sure!"

Jamie visibly relaxed and grinned into his coffee cup.

"Maybe the four of us could go together." Matt looked at me.

I hesitated for a fraction of a second when Llewellyn's face entered my mind. All three of them looked at me. "Ah...as long as the Abernathys don't need me." It wasn't what I wanted to say but I didn't know how to refuse.

"Then it's a date!" Mabel said.

Why couldn't my life be that simple? I wondered. Matt was kind and gentle but he wasn't the one I wanted to be with on New Year's Eve.

I went to bed shortly after dinner so I could be at the Abernathys' early to prepare breakfast. I lay on my back, on my stomach, and then on my side. But sleep wouldn't come.

Llewellyn kept appearing when I closed my eyes. He stood on a coastal steamer, tying down boxes of supplies. An older man threw the mooring line onto the wharf. Llewellyn waved to me as the ship steamed out of the harbour. I tried to recall his brown eyes and the freckles across his nose. My heart jumped when I realized I couldn't picture his face clearly.

Going to the football game as a group of friends was one thing, but a date was something else. I decided to tell Matt about Llewellyn on New Year's Eve.

With that thought, I finally fell asleep.

————◦————

On Christmas Day, I wore my dark green velvet dress to the Abernathys'. Professor Abernathy took my coat at the door and I left my boots on the mat beside the hall closet. Mrs. Abernathy was sitting on the sofa in the living room.

"You look lovely, my dear," she said. "I'll set the table while you prepare breakfast."

"Are you sure?" I held out my hands and helped Mrs. Abernathy to her feet.

"Wrapping presents and setting the table puts me in the Christmas spirit," she replied.

By the time I brought in the breakfast tray, the table had been transformed into a winter wonderland. A round mirror with a crowd of tiny skaters lay in the middle of the white tablecloth. Old-fashioned houses stood around the pond on snow made of cotton batting. More tiny people built snowmen and tobogganed.

"Everything is so beautiful!" I set the tray on a tea trolley and leaned down for a closer look.

Mrs. Abernathy's eyes sparkled. "Charles brings the boxes from the attic and I arrange the pieces."

"You create the magic." He kissed her hand.

"Wheel the tea trolley over here and have some breakfast with us, Ginny," Mrs. Abernathy said. "Tell us how you celebrate Christmas back home."

I joined them at the table and poured tea for all of us.

"We decorate the store in evergreen branches, with big red bows," I told them. "We invite the whole town to sample Nana's baking. Many other families bring cookies and candies. The children have apple cider, the women drink tea, and the men drink rum. When the mummers arrive, everyone sings and dances. The best part is lighting the Christmas pudding after dinner."

"What's a mummer?" Professor Abernathy asked as he buttered a tea biscuit.

"At Christmastime, neighbours go from house to house in costumes, with their faces covered. Often the men dress up in their wives' clothes." I smiled thinking of some of the most elaborate mummers I'd seen. "We give them food and drink while they entertain us with singing, dancing, and recitations, and we have to guess who they are."

Professor Abernathy looked fascinated. "What a lovely custom!"

Mrs. Abernathy nodded. "Our first Christmas was in a one-room apartment."

"With a bathroom down the hall," Professor Abernathy added. "We used a candle as our Christmas tree and placed handmade gifts around it."

"Charles made me a flower box for the window."

"And you knitted me socks, gloves, and a scarf." He reached across the table to hold his wife's hand and she smiled at him.

Since the tea and biscuits were finished, I decided to let them share their memories alone. "I'll clear these dishes away," I said. "You take your time at the table." I filled the trolley and excused myself.

I was just hanging the dishtowel to dry when Mrs. Abernathy walked into the kitchen. She wore a beautiful royal blue silk dress.

"Now I'm ready to open presents!" she said. We linked elbows and joined Professor Abernathy in the living room.

I gave Mrs. Abernathy my English notes. "This way, you can follow the lectures and discussions we had in class, even if you couldn't be there."

Mrs. Abernathy clutched them to her chest. "These are more valuable than gold, Ginny."

They gave me a Christmas bonus. "You can send the money home or use it yourself," Professor Abernathy told me. The three of us knew what I would do with it.

My gift to Professor Abernathy was handmade, but not by me; I had bought soft cotton material and Mabel hemmed the edges.

"Handkerchiefs!" he exclaimed. "I never seem to have one when I need it."

"Time to put the ham in," Mrs. Abernathy said. "Charles, let's help Ginny."

For the next two hours, we sat at the kitchen table. We decorated the ham with pineapple and maraschino cherries before it went into the oven, peeled the vegetables and put them in cold water, and arranged a plate of Mildred's Christmas baking.

Mrs. Abernathy stood up and stretched. "This has been fun but I need to lie down for a while. Do you play gin rummy, my dear?"

"I'm the Harbour Grace champ!"

"Good. Beat the socks off my dear husband—I never can."

At four o'clock, I put the vegetables on to boil. By five, the three of us were holding hands and saying grace at the dining room table. Mrs. Abernathy served her husband and me before she helped herself. Everything smelled delicious, but I was anxious to taste it.

I waited until Mrs. Abernathy had filled her plate before I took a bite of baked ham and mashed potato. *Wow*, I thought. *This is good.* The Abernathys heaped praise on me and I blushed with gratitude.

Mrs. Abernathy had just finished reading *Moby Dick* by Herman Melville. It was one of the books I'd brought her so we discussed it all through dinner.

"I don't understand how someone could be so obsessed with a single idea," she said.

"Look at Malcolm Jones," Professor Abernathy replied. He looked at me. "I'm so sorry, Ginny. I didn't mean to spoil your dinner."

Mrs. Abernathy put down her fork and gave me a sympathetic look. "Is that old poop giving you a hard time?"

"I'm afraid so," I replied. I pushed a piece of ham around my plate, suddenly full.

"In his case, the fruit didn't fall far from the tree," she said.

"What do you mean?" I asked.

"His parents were very strict. Scottish Presbyterians. Conservative to the bone," she explained. "Couldn't accept change or new ideas. Criticized anyone who didn't agree with them."

"His sister, Margaret Anderson, is a lovely lady," Professor Abernathy said, holding his glass with a thoughtful look. "But poor Malcolm got the worst of both his parents."

"But that shouldn't allow him to be an old poop!" Mrs. Abernathy insisted.

"I suppose it shouldn't, but he's an only son," Professor Abernathy reasoned. "And you know how those Scots put all their hopes and dreams into their male offspring."

"All that carrying on the family name nonsense," Mrs. Abernathy said, returning to her mashed potatoes. "It hasn't done Malcolm a bit of good."

I looked from one to the other. "I'm doomed!"

"You told me you did well on his exam," Professor Abernathy said. "That's all you need to guarantee your success."

"I'm sure Charles is right, my dear. Don't you worry."

CHAPTER 20

NEW YEAR'S EVE

————◀○▶————

MABEL ARRIVED BACK AT THE RESIDENCE just before dinner. She said she had a good Christmas visit with her family in Milroy but she was glad to be back in time for the dance. We quickly ate dinner and returned to our room to get ready.

"You can't wear your green velvet dress with *socks* and *school shoes*," Mabel said. "And I only have one pair of stockings." She emerged from her closet wearing the blue satin dress she'd made in her textile class. "You'll have to wear your boots outside and then put on these shoes with bare legs when we get there. Try them on."

I sat on the edge of her bed and slipped on a pair of black shoes with small heels. "They fit!" I stood up and took a few wobbly steps.

"Good. You're all set." Mabel took one last look in the mirror, grabbed her coat, and opened the door for me.

The living room was crowded with young men waiting for their dates. Mabel spotted the Baker boys' blond hair through the crowd and waved. Jamie and Matt joined us in the foyer and we put on our coats.

"You two look beautiful," Jamie said.

"Thanks," Mabel replied.

I felt myself blushing. No one had ever called me beautiful before. I smiled at Matt and we walked out into the falling snow.

At the Union Building, we joined the crowd streaming up the outside steps and through the front doors. Even before we walked up the inside stairs, we saw a huge evergreen tree in the foyer, covered with a thousand lights and shimmering ornaments. We brushed off our coats, stomped the snow off our boots, and joined the others to admire the tree.

In the rooms on either side of the foyer, fires burned in the hearths and people laughed and moved in a kaleidoscope of colour. A band played in the room to our right. People danced in a cleared area in the middle of the floor, while others clapped to the music, or sang along.

Beyond the foyer, the arches over the long hall were hung with evergreen garlands, red ribbons, and pinecones. We walked to the coat check through an enchanted forest, in the middle of which stood tables loaded with sandwiches, cakes, cookies, and bowls of punch.

It reminded me of the store on Christmas Eve when our neighbours dropped in. I imagined seeing Llew in the crowd and when our eyes met, he raised his glass to me and smiled. A feeling of relief swept over me. Soon Matt would know all about him.

"Where would you like to go first?" Matt asked.

"Let's listen to the music," I suggested.

"I'd like to dance," Mabel piped up.

While she and Jamie took to the dance floor, Matt and I sat in a quiet corner and talked about Matt's upcoming graduation in the spring. He told his parents he didn't want a big fuss, maybe just a family dinner.

I asked what he planned to do after graduation but he hadn't made up his mind. Cap Aretz had asked him to stay at Purdue and work as a flight instructor until he knew what he wanted to do next. Matt liked that idea.

After half an hour, Mabel flopped down next to us on the sofa. Her face was flushed and she fanned herself. She and Jamie had been jiving on the crowded dance floor. Although his baby giraffe legs made him look slightly awkward most of the time, on the dance floor Jamie looked like a professional—gliding, dipping, and twirling without missing a beat.

He loosened his tie and looked down at Mabel. "Would you like some punch?"

"Sure!" she replied.

He excused himself but before I could include Mabel in my conversation with Matt, she jumped up again. "I see some of the girls from our floor. Tell Jamie I'll be right back."

Within a few minutes, Jamie carefully wound his way back to where we sat. "Sorry. I could only carry two glasses." He put them on the coffee table and sat down.

"No problem," Matt said. "I'll get some for Ginny and me."

"How was Professor Jones's Christmas dinner?" I asked Jamie. I'd been dying to find out.

"Surprisingly good. He shook our hands as we walked in the door. He wandered around and spoke to each of us individually. We laughed at his jokes and told some of our own."

"That doesn't sound like the Professor Jones I know."

"Jack and I were surprised too." Jamie leaned over and picked up his glass.

"Tell me more."

"If any of the food platters looked empty, he'd go to the kitchen and Mrs. MacDonald would fill them up."

"Who's she?" I asked.

"His housekeeper. Her mother was the housekeeper for his parents."

"What does the house look like?"

"It's full of antiques. Most of them came from Scotland when his grandparents moved to Indiana. The house was left to his parents. He moved back to care for his mother when his father died."

"How do you know all this?"

"I listened to his conversations with the other students—like you told me to."

I chuckled. "You did a great job."

He held up his punch in a mock toast. "Your wish is my command."

Everything Jamie saw confirmed what the Abernathys had told me. Change of any kind had not been a feature in Professor Jones's family. I hoped getting a good mark on his exam was all I needed. I thought further about Jamie's description and realized that Mabel's uncle Malcolm really did exist. When a female wasn't invading his sacred space, he was kind and considerate.

A Benny Goodman song began just as Mabel came back. Jamie jumped up and the two of them headed for the dance floor. Matt asked me to dance but I confessed that I wasn't a very good dancer. He laughed and said we made a perfect pair.

I told him about my job and how much I liked the Abernathys. "She called Professor Jones an old poop."

"Ah, so that's why you like them," Matt said, his blue eyes twinkling with laughter.

"That and more. They're kind people—and they're honest."

Mabel flopped down next to me again. "Let's freshen up."

I sat looking puzzled until Mabel stood, took my hand, and pulled me off the sofa. We walked down the hall and into the ladies' room.

"'Let's freshen up' means let's go to the bathroom?"

"I want to cool off and check my lipstick." Mabel looked in the mirror. Her face was red and shiny. She cupped her hands and splashed cold water on her face. After she dried, she opened a compact and pressed powder on her forehead, nose, and chin. "All I need now is more lipstick. I don't want to be hot and sticky when I kiss Jamie for the first time."

I smiled. "Exactly when do you expect this to happen?"

"At midnight, of course!" Mabel stared at me in the mirror.

All at once I made the connection. New Year's Eve—midnight—Jamie and Mabel—Matt and me. "But I can't kiss Matt, I haven't told him about Llewellyn yet."

"Who?" Mabel turned around to face me.

"A boy back home."

"Is he your…boyfriend?"

"I've never used that exact word but I know I love him, and he loves me."

Mabel was still staring at me like I was an idiot. "What about Matt?"

"We're just friends."

She clapped a hand to her forehead. "Not in his mind!"

I rushed out of the ladies' room and found Matt next to the piano, talking with a group of boys. When he saw me, he excused himself. I asked him if there was a quiet place where we could talk. I followed him to a window seat at the end of the hall and we both sat down.

"I'm sorry I haven't told you this sooner."

"Told me what?"

"There's someone I love in Newfoundland."

Matt paused, digesting this information. "I see," he eventually said.

I rushed to explain, to fill the silence. "His name is Llewellyn Crane. He works in our store sometimes. I've known him since I was seven."

"You grew up together?"

I nodded. "He started working in Papa's store when he was ten."

"Tell me about him."

It was my turn to pause. "Really?"

"Sure."

"When he was first hired, he swept the floors and delivered the groceries. By the time he was fifteen, Papa relied on him for everything." I paused and my eyes filled with tears. "After Papa died, Llewellyn continued working at the store. By that time there was no money to pay him but he showed up anyway. When I ran away to find Amelia, he cared for Mom, Nana, and Billy." I brushed a tear off my cheek. "You just don't forget Llewellyn Crane when you meet someone new."

"I see that," Matt said gently. "Ginny, it's okay."

The countdown to midnight began and I looked up at him.

"Ten, nine, eight—" the crowd chanted.

The lights twinkled in Matt's eyes.

"—four, three, two, one!"

When the clock struck twelve, he leaned over and kissed me on the cheek. I touched my cheek and smiled. Although telling Matt about Llewellyn hadn't gone as planned, I felt as if a heavy load had been lifted.

———◦———

A little while later, the four of us walked back to the residence together. Matt and I arrived at the front steps before Mabel and Jamie.

"Thank you for being so understanding," I said. "Can we still be friends?"

"Of course," Matt replied. "After all, I need someone to remind me to check the float."

I laughed and Matt leaned over and kissed my cheek again. "Good night, Ginny," he said.

When he got to the corner, he turned around and waved. I waved back and walked inside.

I was already in bed when Mabel came in. "Did you get your New Year's kiss?" I asked her.

Mabel smiled. "I did, and it was wonderful, thank you!"

She slipped her coat off and walked to her closet. "How did Matt take the news about Llewellyn?"

I sat up. "He said we could still be friends."

Mabel sat on the end of my bed. "I wish you'd told me about Llewellyn."

I paused and frowned. "Why?"

"I would have encouraged you to tell Matt before now," she said with a sigh. "It's obvious how he feels about you."

That startled me. "Really? I thought we were just good friends."

Mabel rolled her eyes. "Ginny, for someone as smart as you, you sure don't know much about boys!"

CHAPTER 21

MARKS

—◄o►—

SOON, NEW YEAR'S Eve was a memory and classes were beginning again. It had snowed all night. The roads and sidewalks created a challenge.

"Whew, hang on a minute." Mabel bent over to catch her breath. "I don't remember the snow being this deep when I was younger."

"That's because you were playing in it, not trying to get to class by eight thirty."

Mabel stood up and we started moving forward again.

By eight forty, I was seated in a half-empty classroom. Professor Weeks decided to return our English exams. The other students would get theirs when they arrived. The room was silent as he walked from desk to desk. He placed the exams face down.

"Remember, this is a private communication between you and me. Share your mark if you wish, but don't feel compelled to do so."

I turned my paper over—95 percent. I looked up and smiled at Professor Weeks. He nodded and smiled back. Because there were so many students missing, we were allowed to read or chat until the class was over. Jamie got 77 and Jack got 86.

By the end of the week, most of the exams had been returned and my overall average was 93 percent. *So far so good*, I thought. Just Professor Jones's exam left. I walked into the building with my head held high.

Professor Jones strode into the class and dropped the exams on the front counter. "These will be returned at the end of class."

He proceeded to write the words "Power Train" on the blackboard. He underlined them and turned to the engine on the counter.

"The question is: how does the power from the engine get to the wheels? The answer is in this collection of parts—the clutch assembly, the transmission, the drive shaft, and the differential." He pointed to each one as he named it. "Now, watch carefully. You'll be asked to demonstrate this in the shop tomorrow."

I made notes as he talked. Many of the boys looked at the clock as Professor Jones droned on. I was curious about my mark but I could wait. After the exam, I'd told Jamie I would get between 90 and 100.

Five minutes before the end of class, Professor Jones picked up the pile of exams. Everyone perked up.

"I'll return these from the top mark down. When I call your name, come up here."

He went through the whole class without reading my name. I couldn't figure out what was going on. In my mind, I should have been called in the top three.

Finally he said, "Miss Ginny Ross."

I stood up and walked to the front. The sound of snickering followed me up the aisle.

"Aren't as smart as you thought," Professor Jones whispered.

I picked up my paper and walked back to my seat. I took a deep breath and looked at the mark—63 percent. How could that be? I looked at each question. Almost perfect marks. I added the total of each page. Still 63. It didn't make sense.

Then it hit me. There was a page missing. I'd numbered each one, and page five wasn't there. I checked twice, in case the pages were out of order or stuck together. No page five.

"If you have a question about your mark, forget it." Professor Jones closed his books. "I've already checked them twice. Any inquiry will result in a further loss of marks for your impertinence!" With that threat hanging in the air, he picked up his books and walked out the door.

The rest of the class packed up and followed him. But they didn't miss the opportunity to look back at me, with big smiles and whispers.

When the room was empty, I put my hands over my face. It was unthinkable, but Professor Jones had won. As he'd said, "I was gone." I needed 65 percent in order to move on to the next semester.

I was so numb I couldn't think of what to do next. I didn't even notice Jack and Jamie come back into the classroom and rush to my desk.

"What happened?" they asked at the same time.

"There's a page missing from my exam."

"What?" Jamie turned them over one at a time, scanning my answers. "Almost perfect marks on every question."

"How much was page five worth?" I asked.

Jamie flipped through his exam. "Thirty. If you got perfect on those two questions, you would have had a 93."

"That sounds more like it," Jack said grimly. "What are you going to do?"

I put my hands over my face again and tried to think. What came into my mind was my family, the "Ode to Newfoundland," and the whole town coming out to wish me well when I left for Purdue. "Remember you're our Amelia Earhart, Gin," Llewellyn had shouted as he ran beside the train. I couldn't let them down—I wouldn't let them down. *Think*, I told myself, *think*.

"You heard what Professor Jones said about asking questions." I stood up and put on my coat. "I'll have to go to Dean Potter before Professor Jones claims I forgot to hand in the page."

The three of us ran around the corner to the Engineering Administration Building. Dean Potter's office was on the main floor but his secretary wasn't at her desk. I knocked on his door. When he opened it, he seemed surprised to see me. "Yes?" he said.

"Hello, Dean Potter," I said. "I'm Ginny Ross. I have a problem."

"I suppose you'd better come in and tell me about it."

I sat down and folded my coat over my knees. I waited until he resumed his seat.

"Professor Jones lost a page of my exam."

"That is serious. Let's get him in here."

"He said if we questioned him about our exam, we'd lose more marks."

Dean Potter frowned. "I see. Then I'll do the asking."

He dialled a number and asked Professor Jones to join us. I hoped Jamie and Jack heard him and left the secretary's desk. I crossed my fingers under my coat. Dean Potter asked about my other marks. He'd just finished writing them down when Professor Jones walked in without knocking. Dean Potter explained why I was there.

"Sit down, Malcolm," he said. "I'm concerned about this missing page because Ginny's marks on all her other exams are excellent."

"I was puzzled myself," Professor Jones said, not looking at me. "I can't understand how she could be so careless."

I faced Professor Jones. "You know I could have answered those two questions on page five."

"I know nothing of the kind. I do know in thirty years of teaching I have never lost any part of any exam."

Dean Potter sighed and folded his hands on the desk. "I'm afraid Professor Jones is right, Miss Ross. Why would he lose one page from one particular exam after thirty years?"

"Look," I pointed to the exam in front of him. "The pages are numbered and page five is missing."

"I don't know what you expect me to say." Dean Potter shrugged and held his hand toward Professor Jones. "It's your word against a man who has taught here for thirty years."

I couldn't believe what I was hearing. The dean was agreeing with Professor Jones. Everyone knew he thought women should be kept out of engineering. That's why he lost one page from one particular exam. But somehow I knew I shouldn't say that out loud.

I stood and reached for my exam. "I see," I said.

And I walked out.

CHAPTER 22

LAST RESORT

————◀○▶————

I KNEW I had no time to waste. I ran down the front steps. Jamie and Jack waited on the sidewalk. I told them what had happened in the dean's office. "I have to see the president right away."

"Do you really think that's a good idea?" Jack asked. "You'll be going behind Dean Potter's back and that could get you into more trouble."

"I just failed out of mechanical engineering. How much worse can it get?" I turned and ran down the sidewalk, dodging icy puddles as I went. The boys followed and Jamie explained to Jack what Ed had told us about needing 65 percent to move on to the next semester. Jack wondered why the requirement wasn't better known.

"I suppose the university assumes if you can get into mechanical engineering, you can get 65 percent in the first semester," Jamie replied.

"I'm still not sure she should be going to the *president*," Jack said.

"What else can she do?" Jamie asked.

Jack shrugged. The three of us kept running.

Five minutes later, we reached the president's office. I paused to catch my breath, walked up to the secretary's desk, and asked to see President Elliott.

"He's just about to go home for lunch," she said. "Let me ask if he'll see you. May I have your name?"

"Ginny Ross."

President Elliott came out of his office. "How nice to see you again, Ginny," he said warmly. "Please come in."

The secretary took my coat and hat. I turned to the boys and said I would see them later. Then I followed President Elliott into his office. I sat in the chair he'd pulled out for me in front of his desk. After I explained why I was there, he picked up his phone.

"Dean Potter, please. President Elliott calling." A pause. "Albert, how are you? That's good to hear. I wonder if you could drop by my office?" Another pause. "Now, actually. Yes, right now." He nodded. "Thanks, Albert."

President Elliott hung up and grabbed a notepad. "What are your other marks, Ginny?" He wrote them down.

"I'm not a tattletale but I didn't know where else to go," I said.

"You came to the right place," he reassured me. "This needs to be investigated."

"Thank you," I whispered.

"Have you heard about Amelia's new plane?" President Elliott asked.

"She told me the university bought it for her. She calls it her 'flying laboratory' but I'm not sure how she plans to use it."

"It's a very exciting project. You'll hear about it soon."

A knock on the door ended our conversation. The secretary announced Dean Potter. He walked into the room but stopped when he saw me.

"Albert, please come in." President Elliott pulled another chair in front of his desk. "I understand you've met Miss Ross."

"Ah...yes." He pulled on the knot in his tie, glanced at me, and sat down. Before speaking, he cleared his throat. "I've already explained to Miss Ross that there is nothing we can do."

President Elliott ignored that and turned to me. "When was the exam returned?"

"This morning, sir."

"Where have you been since then?"

"Dean Potter's office and here."

"Were the answers discussed in class?"

"No, sir."

"Did you look at anyone else's exam?"

"No, sir."

Although the questions were rapid fire, the president's tone and demeanour remained relaxed, almost friendly. He needed information and he needed it quickly in order to make a decision. I hadn't wanted to complain about Professor Jones when Mrs. Elliott asked what I would change at Purdue, but I had way too much to lose if I didn't speak up now.

President Elliott sat back and rested his elbows on the arms of the chair. He tapped his fingers together while he thought. "We'll have her write a makeup exam in here in one hour." He buzzed his secretary and asked her to send for his wife.

"Do you realize what a dangerous precedent this sets?" Dean Potter demanded. He grasped the edge of the president's desk and leaned forward in his chair. "Students will be 'losing pages' all over the place!"

"I understand your concern, Albert, but there are just too many coincidences in this case. Sit back and listen."

The dean pushed himself back onto the chair and crossed his arms over his chest.

"All her marks are over 90 percent, except for Malcolm's class," the president said. "If the page hadn't been lost, she could have had a 93 on his exam. This would be consistent with her other marks." Here he paused. "I find it interesting that she missed the cut-off percentage to move on to second semester by two percentage points."

"Are you doubting Malcolm's word?"

"We both know how he feels about females in engineering, Albert."

"But...he'd never go this far."

A knock on the door silenced everyone. Mrs. Elliott walked in and greeted each of us. She raised her eyebrows and looked at her husband.

"I wonder if you'd bring my lunch here?"

"Of course. Would you like extra for Ginny and Albert?"

"Yes. And actually, Malcolm Jones will be here too."

Mrs. Elliott nodded. "No problem. Give me half an hour."

President Elliott picked up the phone and asked for Professor Jones. He invited him to come over for lunch.

Professor Jones arrived ten minutes later. The secretary showed him in. When he saw me, he stopped.

"I might have known you would sneak behind my back," he sneered.

"Come in and sit down, Malcolm," the president said politely but firmly. He passed a pen and a stack of papers across the desk. "We were just discussing Miss Ross's exam for your class. It seems a page has gotten lost in the shuffle. So I'd like you to write a makeup exam for Miss Ross of equal length and difficulty as the one she originally wrote."

"What!" Professor Jones's face turned red and his forehead glistened with moisture.

"I've explained my concerns to Albert," the president said.

Professor Jones turned to Dean Potter. "And you agreed with this?"

"Well, ah... it couldn't hurt, Malcolm."

"So, my thirty-year record is worth nothing?" he shouted.

There was silence in the room. Then Professor Jones pointed his finger at the president. "I'll do this. But you will have my letter of resignation in the morning!"

"Let's finish with the exam and talk when Miss Ross leaves," the president said.

Professor Jones glared at me, picked up the pen and paper, and sat at a long table under the windows. Everyone jumped when Mrs. Elliott opened the door. She walked in with a tray of sandwiches and a plate of celery, carrots, and pickles. The secretary followed her with tea and coffee. The two of them passed the food and drinks around before they left. The silence was broken only by the occasional crunch of a carrot or celery stick. I could hardly swallow a thing.

After twenty minutes, Professor Jones stood up and walked to the president's desk. He threw the new exam in front of him. President Elliott thanked him and asked if he had a class that afternoon. He asked Dean Potter the same question. When he knew they were free, he handed each of them a booklet.

"This is the new course outline for 1937–38. Please read the information on mechanical engineering and make any changes you wish. You may as well do that here while Miss Ross writes her exam."

Neither of them looked very happy. Each took a few more sandwiches and refilled his coffee cup. Dean Potter sat in a chair in the corner. I sat at the long table by the window. President Elliott remained at his desk. Professor Jones chose one of the chairs in front of the desk. But he turned it away from the president before he sat down.

An hour later, I handed my exam to President Elliott. He told me I was free to leave.

As I closed the door, the shouting began.

CHAPTER 23

LETTER

---◄○►---

I HAD MISSED Professor Abernathy's class to write the makeup exam. I quickly walked to his house because I knew he and Mrs. Abernathy would be worried. Professor Abernathy answered the door and shouted over his shoulder, "She's here!"

Before I could pull off my boots, he led me into the living room. Mrs. Abernathy sat on the sofa. "My dear, we were so worried." She patted the spot next to her.

Professor Abernathy took my hat and coat before I sat down. He sat in the chair opposite us and I described the whole day. They didn't say a word until I finished.

"That old *poop*! Do you know anything about this, Charles?"

"I haven't heard a word, my dear."

Mrs. Abernathy shook her head and squeezed my hand. As if on cue, the phone rang and Professor Abernathy answered it. He only spoke for a few minutes before he hung up.

"There's an emergency meeting of the mechanical engineering department at eight o'clock tonight," he said.

"What does that mean?" I asked.

"It means the president has something he wants to discuss with us."

"My makeup exam?"

"Possibly. But try not to worry about it. He may have…other information he wants to share with us."

I nodded and Mrs. Abernathy squeezed my hand again. "We're here for you, my dear."

I leaned over and kissed her cheek. "Thank you. And now I'd better get home. Mabel will wonder where I am." I stood up.

Professor Abernathy held my coat while I slipped my arms in. I pulled on my hat and turned to him. "If I come to your office early tomorrow, will you tell me what happened at the meeting?"

"Of course," he assured me.

I said goodbye and walked to the residence in the fading light. The snowbanks along the road were grey, the bare trees were grey, and my mood was grey. It had been a long day.

When I opened my mailbox, my mood brightened. A letter from Llewellyn! So far I'd only received a Christmas card because he was always at sea. I enjoyed hearing from my family and friends, but this letter was special. I raced upstairs to read it, tearing the envelope open as I went.

> *Dear Ginny,*
> *I met the most wonderful girl. Her name is Edwina Collier. She lives in Burgeo. Her dad works on the steamer with me. When*

we pulled in there to deliver supplies, he took me home for dinner. And there she was. She has blonde, curly hair and blue eyes. She's 15 years old. Her dad told me she's too young to walk out with me. I have to wait until she grows up a bit. I guess he saw the look on my face when I first saw her. I'll keep you posted on this new development in my life.

I hope you're still loving school.

Your friend, Llewellyn

I couldn't move. All the energy drained out of my body. I heard the girls filing into the dining room. A few said hi, but I didn't answer.

Someone touched my arm. "Are you coming into dinner?" Mabel asked.

I didn't answer so she took the letter from my hand.

She was quiet as she scanned the page. "Llewellyn met a girl?"

Hearing the words made them true. Tears ran down my cheeks.

"Oh, Ginny," Mabel said, as she wiped my tears with her sleeve and looked around. "Come on." She led me up to our room. She took off my coat and hat, sat me on the bed, and pulled off my boots. "Stay here. I'll say you're not feeling well and bring you back some tea."

Tears dripped off my chin onto my blouse. My nose ran onto my upper lip. I couldn't move.

Mabel returned with a pot of tea and two cups. She held one out but I still couldn't move.

"How could he do this?" I looked up at her.

Mabel shrugged and poured the tea. "Take this. It's hot, be careful."

I took the cup and blew on the tea. "I thought he loved me."

Mabel put her teacup on my bedside table and sat down beside me. "What made you think that?"

"He was my best friend. We talked about everything. We would never tell each other's secrets. He cradled Papa's head on his lap while I ran for Doc Cron." I sniffed, wiped my nose on my sleeve, and took a sip of tea. "After Papa's funeral, he was always there for us—finding coal on the railroad tracks, hunting rabbits, and catching cod. He shared whatever he got between his family and ours."

"Did he ever kiss you?" Mabel asked.

"Lots of times."

"Where?"

"Mostly in the store. When he was saying goodbye."

Mabel rolled her eyes. "No, where on you—your lips?"

"He held my face in his hands and kissed my forehead, like Papa used to do."

Mabel stood and picked up her teacup. She walked to the window and turned around. For a minute or so she sipped in silence.

I continued to sniff. "What are you thinking?"

She sighed. "You're not going to like it."

"Tell me anyway."

Mabel took another sip of tea before she answered. "I don't want to say this, but here goes. Llewellyn loved you. But not like a boyfriend."

"But he kissed me!"

"He kissed you like Papa used to." Mabel waited, but when I didn't reply, she continued. "Llewellyn thought of himself as Papa, loving and protecting you."

"A few kisses from Jamie Baker and now you're the expert!" I shot back. I splashed tea down the front of my blouse when I stood up.

Mabel pursed her lips and shrugged. "I knew you wouldn't like it."

"Then why did you say it?"

"My grandma says the truth will set you free."

"What am I free from? I just lost a boyfriend."

"You're free to have a best friend in Newfoundland, instead of living with a—" she caught herself.

I looked up. "Living with a what?"

"Misunderstanding." She pushed herself off the windowsill. "You know so much about engines and planes, I forget how little you know about boys."

"You've already pointed that out!" I curled up on my bed, faced the wall, and pulled the bedspread around me, blocking out Mabel, blocking out Llew's letter, and blocking out my embarrassment.

CHAPTER 24

WORN OUT

————◄○►————

"MY DEAR, YOU look terrible." It was eight o'clock the next morning. Professor Abernathy stood up and pulled a chair over to his desk. "You mustn't let this Professor Jones business worry you. I know dealing with him is difficult, but you are making history."

"I don't want to make history. I just want to pass first year engineering, get my pilot's licence, and support my family." I sank down on the chair. "It wasn't supposed to be this hard once I got to Purdue."

"Now, now, my dear. This is no time to lose hope. Slip off your coat and sit back. I have a lot to tell you." Professor Abernathy sat down and leaned toward me. He told me the meeting didn't end until ten o'clock. There was shouting, desk thumping, and fist waving.

"Wait! Don't go so fast," I said. "Tell me everything."

"Yes, of course—sorry." He smiled and rubbed his hands together. "First, the president reminded us that the Women's

Residence just opened a year ago. And that the university had hired Amelia Earhart as a part-time career counsellor for women and an aviation advisor; he said her courage and success as a pilot made her a role model for female students. All of this was done to attract more women to higher education. Including women in all subject areas could place Purdue at the forefront of modern education."

I moved to the edge of my chair. "But Professor Jones isn't doing that."

"Precisely." Professor Abernathy sat back and smiled.

"Did President Elliott use my name?" I asked.

"He spoke in generalities about females in non-traditional subjects. He said his information came from students other than the female students themselves."

"He's probably referring to Ed." I sat back and for a few seconds tried to picture the meeting before I continued. "Did President Elliott mention how Professor Jones treats me?"

Professor Abernathy told me that the president gave three examples without naming the professor: seating female students in the back away from the others, ignoring a raised hand to answer, and making humiliating comments designed to make the other students laugh. That was when some professors shouted, "Shame, shame!"

Professor Abernathy clasped his hands and said the best was yet to come. Professor Jones gave himself away when his face turned bright red. That confirmed what most people already knew.

"Did anyone side with him?" I asked.

"Dean Potter and a few other professors you haven't met yet. That's when the shouting and desk thumping started."

"How did it end? The suspense is killing me!"

"The president explained his reasons for the makeup exam. He asked for a vote of confidence from the student's teachers. Dean Potter insisted that the whole Mechanical Engineering Department should vote, since it affected all of us."

I stood up and walked to the window. "But...if President Elliott did that, wouldn't Dean Potter and Professor Jones have more support?"

"They got some but not enough! Your case goes to the Board of Trustees."

"They're the ones who approved the purchase of Amelia's flying laboratory!"

He sat back in his chair, crossed his arms, and smiled. "Precisely."

———◦———

I walked into Professor Weeks's class at 8:20. Jamie and Jack rushed up to me.

"Are you all right?" Jamie asked.

My eyes were swollen, my hair was flattened, and my clothes were wrinkled. "It's been a long night," I said. "But I'm feeling a bit better."

"What happened when you saw the president?"

"My meeting was good, but I'm too tired to explain everything right now."

They told me that was fine. Professor Weeks walked in and we sat down. I put my elbows on the desk and my chin in my hands. I closed my eyes and listened to him reading a poem by Edgar Allen Poe:

> I was a child and she was a child
> In this kingdom by the sea,
> But we loved with a love that was more than a love
> I and my Annabel Lee.

The lump in my throat grew larger. I didn't think I had any tears left but there they were just the same. Mabel was right, I thought. There was no use living with a misunderstanding. But that didn't ease the pain in my chest.

Two days after the emergency mechanical engineering meeting, Professor Jones swept into the class. He dropped his books on the counter. "Raise your hand if you think you could have done better on my exam."

For a few seconds no one moved. Then one hand went up, two more followed, until six hands were raised.

"I think you should all march straight over to the president's office," Professor Jones said. "Demand to write a makeup exam!"

The boys looked at each other but no one moved.

"It's easy," he said. "Ask Ginny how she did it."

A chorus of voices replied, "What! That's not fair! What makes her so special?"

"I'll leave those questions for you to answer, gentlemen. In the meantime, I have a class to teach."

Throughout the lesson, one boy or another turned around and glared at me. And that was how the classes went, day after day. Professor Jones had managed to divide the students into two groups: a small group who supported me, and a large group who supported him.

The weeks dragged on. The pain from Llewellyn's letter was fading. But every now and then a feeling of emptiness washed over me.

Three months until school ended. I wondered if I could hang on.

CHAPTER 25

NEWS

————◄○►————

M ABEL WALKED INTO our room and hung up her coat. "Have you checked your mailbox lately?"

"I'm afraid to." I closed the book on my desk and turned around.

"I can see at least one letter through the glass."

"It can wait."

"What if it's good news? You're due for some."

"That's true." I stood up and stretched. "Don't leave. You'll miss my good news."

Mabel chuckled and sat down at her desk.

I slowly walked down to the mailboxes. I peeked through the glass door on mine and saw Amelia's handwriting on a thick envelope. I dropped my keys on the floor twice before I managed to open the lock. No time to get upstairs. I tore open the envelope.

Dear Ginny,

I'm afraid George and I have been keeping a secret. My next flight will be around the world. That's why I needed my "flying laboratory." Fortunately, Purdue supplied it.

It's true that others have already accomplished this—Wiley Post for one. He flew the shortest route. I intend to fly the longest distance: at the equator—27,000 miles!

I need permission to land in all the foreign countries on my flight. Then there are all the arrangements necessary to refuel. George has been working on this for months. I've even written to President Roosevelt for help.

If all goes well, I'll be in San Francisco, California, on March 17. My first stop will be Honolulu, Hawaii. Then the route will be east to west—Howland Island will be next.

I'm taking navigators with me as far as Howland Island. It's a tiny dot in the Pacific Ocean. Fred Noonan is a former navigator on the Pan American Airlines Pacific route. He's made a dozen or so trips. He also has experience with celestial navigation from a plane. Harry Manning will join us. He's also a navigator. The more eyes we have on board to find that dot, the better.

I think I have just one more long flight in my system. Then I'll settle down in my lovely home in North Hollywood to enjoy the California sunshine, books, and friends. I'll always be involved in aviation in some way. But I'll be 40 years old on my next birthday. It's time to let you younger ones take over!

We'll keep you posted. George sends his best. You are often in our thoughts. After my trip, you and Mabel can come to see us in California.

Affectionately, A

I ran upstairs and swung the door open.

"You're not going to believe this!"

I hurried across the room and laid the letter on Mabel's desk.

She read for a couple of minutes and let out a yell. I put my finger to my lips.

"Shh! Not so loud."

"Sorry," Mabel whispered, passing the letter back to me. "I don't know if I'm more excited about her flight or seeing her in California." She jumped up, grabbed her coat, and ran out of the room. "I'll be right back," she shouted over her shoulder.

I walked to the window and leaned my forehead against the pane. The snowbanks had dropped in the last few days and water ran down the driveway. Patches of sun shone through the clouds. I closed my eyes and lifted my face to the warmth coming through the glass.

I read Amelia's letter again. One more long flight and then she wanted to settle down. That was what stood out in my mind. I couldn't imagine Amelia without a new adventure luring her into the sky. I folded the letter carefully and put it in my desk drawer with her other ones.

The door flew open and Mabel rushed back in. She passed a large book to me and shrugged off her coat.

"Open it to page fifty-seven," she instructed.

I laid the book on my desk—an atlas. I flipped the pages and knew instantly what Mabel had in mind.

"We can follow Amelia on this map!"

"As soon as we know her full route, we can trace the map on poster paper, mark her stops, and hang it on our wall," Mabel replied. "It'll be like a newsreel right here in our room!"

Amelia hadn't been in touch with us for a few months, and now we knew why. We put the atlas on the floor and each of us traced half the world map. We were almost finished when Mabel glanced at the clock.

"I have to go," she said, gathering her coat and hat. "It's time for me to clean Uncle Malcolm's den."

She'd done this before so I knew she wouldn't be gone very long.

———◦———

When the door opened about an hour later, I turned around in my chair.

"I finished your part. What colour do you think—" I stopped when I saw Mabel's face. "What's wrong?"

Mabel just shook her head and walked toward me. She laid a piece of scorched paper on my desk. I picked it up.

"My missing page five! Where did you find it?"

"In the fireplace in Uncle Malcolm's den. There was a clump of partially burned paper in the middle of the ashes. I recognized your handwriting." She put her hands over her mouth to muffle the sobs.

I jumped up and put my arms around her. When her shoulders shook, I held her tighter.

Slowly the crying stopped and Mabel whispered, "Oh, Ginny, I'm so, so sorry."

I patted her back. "It's okay."

Mabel stood back and looked into my eyes. "No, it's not. What he did is unforgivable. How could he be so kind to me and so cruel to you?"

"Because you're behaving the way you should, and I'm not."

"What do you mean?" Mabel sniffed and dabbed her eyes with an embroidered hanky.

I took her hand and we sat on my bed. "You're studying home economics and I'm studying engineering."

Mabel nodded. "And women 'don't belong' in engineering."

"According to him."

"That's no excuse!" Mabel cried. "And I'm going to tell him so."

I stood up and walked to the window. There was the issue of Mabel's tuition to be considered. I turned around and paused, looking for the words that would make her feel better.

"Look, we know the truth," I said. "That's all that matters."

"I just can't wrap my head around the fact that he hid his true nature for so long. I always thought I was a pretty good judge of character."

"You have to remember that you only saw him in family settings, where he was a kind and generous man."

Mabel jumped to her feet. "I don't want his tuition money, if that's what you're thinking. I'll apply for a scholarship before I take another cent from him!"

"Can your brothers get scholarships?"

Mabel slumped back down on the bed. "I don't know, but there are only so many scholarships to go around. I can't imagine them giving three to one family."

"Then you have your answer."

"What if the trustees won't accept your makeup exam?"

"I'll have to trust President Elliott. He wants women in non-traditional subjects as much as we do."

I walked to my desk, tore up the page, and threw the pieces in the wastebasket.

Mabel stood up and dried her eyes on her sleeve. "Thanks, roomie," she whispered. She slipped off her coat and looked at the map.

I suggested hanging it on the wall and held out Amelia's letter. "We can mark her starting point and her first few stops."

Mabel smiled and nodded. She took a box of crayons out of her desk drawer. "We use these in clothing design but they'll work just as well on the map."

"You look for San Francisco and Honolulu. I'll look for Howland Island…if it's even on this map," I said.

"Why wouldn't it be?"

"It's awfully small."

CHAPTER 26

AT LAST

———◄◦►———

A WEEK LATER, someone knocked on our door. Joanne, one of the girls from Mabel's textile class, poked her head in. "Note for Ginny from Miss Schleman."

I was lying on my bed reading so I sat up and held out my hand. "Thanks, Joanne."

Joanne smiled and closed the door behind her.

"What's up?" Mabel asked.

I scanned the note. "President Elliott wants to see me in Miss Schleman's office."

I jumped up, tucked in my blouse, and ran down the stairs. Just as I reached the foyer, President Elliott and Miss Schleman walked out of her office.

"Let's see what Mrs. Phillips has for an afternoon snack," she said, turning to me.

We walked through the dining room to the kitchen, where Mrs. Phillips was closing the oven door.

"Oatmeal raisin cookies in ten minutes, my loves," she said. She stood up and saw President Elliott. "Oh, my Lord! I've just called the president my love." She put her hand over her mouth and turned a deeper shade of red.

We all burst out laughing, including Mrs. Phillips.

"Oatmeal raisin are my favourite," President Elliott said.

He sat down at the kitchen table and invited us to join him. "You'll want to hear this too, Mrs. Phillips. You're part of the girls' lives at Purdue." She took off her apron and sat down.

He explained that the Board of Trustees had met that afternoon. My makeup exam was on the agenda. I crossed my fingers on both hands and held my breath.

"They unanimously approved your makeup exam, Ginny. You got 96 percent, which gives you an overall average of 94. You stood first in your class."

He held out his hand and I shook it.

Like a balloon slowly losing air, all the tension from the last few months left my body. Miss Schleman shook my hand and Mrs. Phillips gave me a warm hug. "This calls for a celebration!" she said. "Cookies and tea for everyone."

I turned to President Elliott. "Thank you for all your support."

"Thank *you* for not giving up," he said. "Many young women have done just that. You Newfoundlanders are made of strong stuff!"

Mrs. Phillips filled our cups and then put a big plate of warm cookies in the middle of the table. "Life doesn't get any better than this," President Elliott said, and we all agreed.

As we ate, I answered questions about Newfoundland—where I lived, who was in my family, and how I had learned so much about aviation.

"What do you miss most?" President Elliott asked.

"The smell of the sea," I replied. "When you're born by the sea, it holds you forever."

"I feel the same about Indiana cornfields!" Miss Schleman said.

"Speaking of Indiana cornfields, I'd better get back to work," President Elliott added.

We thanked Mrs. Phillips for her hospitality before we stood up. Then I asked to be excused to tell Mabel the good news.

"May I have a word before you go, Ginny?" President Elliott asked.

Miss Schleman and Mrs. Phillips excused themselves.

"To protect the integrity of your makeup exam, Dean Potter marked it. I told Professor Jones about your new mark and he was not pleased. Don't hesitate to tell me if he gives you a hard time."

I smiled. "I will, thank you."

I ran upstairs and in one breath told Mabel the news. In the next breath, I asked her to pick up the boys. "I'll meet you in the coffee shop in half an hour." I grabbed my coat and ran out.

No one answered when I knocked on the Abernathys' front door. *Mildred must be out shopping*, I thought. I opened the door and shouted, "Hello?"

"In the kitchen!" came the answer. The Abernathys sat at the table, a chessboard between them.

"I stood first in the class!"

They both clapped and Mrs. Abernathy reached up for a hug. Professor Abernathy stood up and shook my hand. "I knew you could do it."

"Sit down and give us all the details," Mrs. Abernathy said.

After I finished describing the sequence of events, Professor Abernathy turned to his wife. "I do believe we're seeing a monumental change at Purdue. Not only at the board level but also among the faculty. I told Ginny she was making history, my dear."

"And so she is," Mrs. Abernathy replied.

She squeezed my hand and invited me to stay for dinner. I explained that Mabel, Jamie, Jack, Matt, and Ed were waiting for me at the coffee shop. Mrs. Abernathy told me I must go at once and share the good news.

At the door Professor Abernathy thanked me for coming there first. "I know Clara appreciated hearing the news from you." He shook my hand and told me to come back soon. I jumped down the front steps and began running again.

When I arrived at the coffee shop, Matt waved from our usual booth. I wound through the tables and squeezed in next to Mabel.

"What did President Elliott say?" Jamie asked.

"I stood first in the class!"

The table erupted in a cheer. Everyone in the coffee shop looked at us. Mabel hugged me and the boys shook my hand.

Matt held my hand a little longer than the others. "How about a round of root beer to celebrate?" he suggested.

"Are you paying?" Jamie asked.

Matt rolled his eyes. "Don't I always?"

"Then count me in," Jamie said with a laugh.

"Wait," I said, and then I had to stop. I felt the tears rising to the surface again. I took a deep breath and continued. "I couldn't have done it without all of you. When the going got tough, you were always there for me. You wouldn't let me lose hope and for that I'll always be grateful." I brushed a tear off my cheek.

I looked around the table at the smiling faces—Mabel, Matt, Jamie, Jack, and Ed. *What a day*, I thought. *If I can survive the rest of Professor Jones's class and write a good final exam, I'm home free.*

CHAPTER 27

SET BACK

————◄o►————

I WONDERED HOW Professor Jones would react to the results of my makeup exam. But I didn't have to wait long. On Monday morning he walked into class smiling and rubbing his hands together. The class grew silent.

He swept his arm toward me in a theatrical manner. "Please join me in congratulating Ginny. Much to my surprise, she has managed—and I do mean managed—to stand first in the class."

The usual rumble of angry voices replied. Professor Jones just stood behind the counter smiling and nodding. He got the reaction he had been hoping for. He let the noise grow to an alarming level before he raised his hand. The boys who were standing sat down and the grumbling slowly subsided.

"I thought Bill Troost stood first," one of the boys said.

"That was before Ginny wrote her makeup exam," Professor Jones replied. He turned to Bill. "Apparently you're now second."

Bill shrugged as if he didn't care, but some of the others turned to me and shouted, "That's not fair!" and "Cheater!"

I didn't know where to look or how to look. I didn't want to look afraid or, worse, happy. Looking at my desk seemed like the safest thing to do. Eventually, the noise stopped and I glanced up. Professor Jones had raised his hand again. He announced they'd better get started if they wanted to finish the course before the exam.

Find your own path and stick to it, I repeated, whenever one of the boys turned around and scowled at me. As soon as the class was over, I got out of there as fast as I could.

—◇—

Finally, the weekend arrived and with it, a change in the weather. Water from the melting snow ran down the streets and the sun felt warm on the tops of our heads as Matt and I walked to the Luna Theater. Amelia's around-the-world flight was to be featured on the newsreel.

Matt bought our popcorn and we sat down just as the newsreel began. "Miss Amelia Earhart has announced the date of her historical flight." The reporter held a microphone toward Amelia.

"I'll fly from California to Hawaii on March 15. Then on to Howland Island. From there to Australia and India, across Africa to South America, and on to New York."

"What is the purpose of your flight?"

"I want to research the effect of long-distance flights on humans and machines."

"Does this flight have anything to do with your belief that women are as capable as men?"

"Of course!"

Matt squeezed my hand. "Not long till takeoff," he whispered. I smiled and squeezed back.

On the way home, we talked about Amelia's flight and Professor Jones's reaction to my first-place standing. But there was something else on my mind. My steps slowed and I stopped.

"I have something to tell you…about Llewellyn."

"Okay."

I hesitated when I felt my face getting hot. I had been so wrong about Llewellyn that it was hard to talk about him without feeling embarrassed. I cleared my throat.

"Llewellyn found a girlfriend."

"Another girlfriend?"

"Well, actually, Mabel helped me understand that I was his best friend, not his girlfriend. Technically, Edwina Collier is Llewellyn's first girlfriend."

Matt smiled, "You're taking it very well."

"Not at first—but what can I do? It's better to live with the truth than a misunderstanding."

"Very wise."

"Mabel was the one who said that, not me."

We burst out laughing. "I'm sure you're wise too," Matt said.

I linked my arm with Matt's and we continued our walk to the residence. I was amazed at how easily we talked and laughed together. I wondered if we'd always been like that but I had been too focused on Llewellyn to see it. What was it Nana used to say, when one door closes another one opens? I gave Matt's arm a squeeze and smiled up at him.

—◦—

Over the next few days, the excitement about Amelia's flight grew. The girls in the residence arrived nightly to look at the map in our room.

"Flying over the ocean is so much more difficult," Faye said. "You don't know where you are."

"And it's a land plane," Barb added. "What happens if they run out of fuel?"

"Land plane or not, how are they supposed to land in the dense jungles in India, Africa, or South America?" Joan asked.

One night, about a week later, Miss Schleman brought Mrs. Phillips in to see the map. Although it hadn't been marked yet, I traced Amelia's proposed route with my finger.

"That distance is beyond my understanding." Mrs. Phillips shook her head. "I'll stick to my kitchen and my oatmeal raisin cookies, which, by the way, are cooling right now."

We gave Mrs. Phillips a cheer and followed her and Miss Schleman downstairs.

Mabel and I had been following Amelia's updates on the Abernathys' radio and the newsreels at the movies. Then another source of information became available. The student newspaper, the *Purdue Exponent*, was given special permission by the *New York Herald Tribune* to run their reports about Amelia's flight. After a delay caused by dangerous winds, Amelia had finally taken off from Oakland, California. Every table in the dining room had at least one newspaper on it.

At our table, Sarah read aloud: "Bulletin: Oakland, California, March 17—Special. Three hours and 16 min. after she took off on the first leg of her world flight (9:13 PM CST), Amelia Earhart radioed, "All is well. Plane acting fine." Although her exact position was not given, she is reported to be 365 miles offshore en route to Honolulu."

Everyone at the table cheered.

After dinner, Mabel drew a black line from Oakland, California, toward Honolulu, Hawaii. "We'll complete the line when she gets there," Mabel said to the girls who were filing into our room. We left the door open while we did our homework so others could wander in and look at the map.

The next day, March 19, there were two articles at dinner: "Amelia Five Minutes Ahead of Schedule; Gives Vivid Description of 2,400 Mile Hop." Amelia had written this article as soon as the trio landed in Honolulu, at 5:29 A.M. local time. She intended to take off on the next leg of her flight the same night. However, that wasn't possible. The second article explained why. "Amelia Earhart Awaits Favourable Weather Reports Before Making 1,800 Mile Flight to Howland Island."

Back in our room Mabel completed the line to Honolulu. "Should I start the line to Howland Island?" She turned and looked at me.

"Let's wait until she's getting close, like we did with Honolulu."

On March 20, the Elliotts joined Mabel, the boys, and me at the Abernathys' for the news report on Amelia's takeoff from Honolulu. Professor Abernathy tuned the radio from bursts of static to a sombre male voice. "Early this morning, Amelia Earhart crashed her flying laboratory while taking off from Luke Field in Honolulu, Hawaii."

My hands flew up to my mouth. Everyone else leaned forward. "Fortunately, Miss Earhart cut the engines and avoided a fire. She, Fred Noonan, and Harry Manning walked away without a scratch. I can't say the same for the aircraft. I have Mr. Paul Mantz with me. He is an advisor to Miss Earhart. Can you describe what happened, Paul?"

"Fred and Harry boarded the plane. Harry started the engines and Amelia joined them ten minutes later. She started her takeoff run and was gaining speed when the plane seemed to pull to the right. She tried to drop power on the left engine to straighten it but it started swinging left. This put all the weight on the right landing gear and it collapsed. The plane skidded on its belly, in a shower of sparks."

"How did you feel watching this?"

"Completely helpless! I've never been more relieved in my life than when I saw the three of them walk away from the plane."

"What will happen to the plane now, Paul?"

"My understanding is it will be brought by ship to the Lockheed plant in Burbank, California, for repair."

"There you have it folks, from an eyewitness to the crash."

Professor Abernathy turned off the radio. The room remained silent. I sat with my fists clenched in my lap.

"At least they're safe," President Elliott said.

"Do you think Amelia will try again?" Mrs. Elliott asked.

"Knowing Amelia, it will take a herd of wild horses to hold her back!" Mabel replied.

CHAPTER 28

NOT ALONE

———◄o►———

THE NEXT DAY life got back to normal, or as normal as it ever got in Professor Jones's class. He walked in, dropped his books on the counter, and crossed his arms over his chest.

"I'm thinking of retiring in June," he announced.

The usual angry rumble of voices was the boys' reply. Then one of the bullies from the front steps stood up and pointed at me. "This is all *your* fault."

"Yeah! It's because of you," someone else added.

More boys joined in. From somewhere a pencil flew across the room and hit me in the face. I touched my cheek and looked at a small smear of blood on my fingers.

Jack stood up and walked across the front of the class. Before he remembered to tuck his tie into his shirt, he grabbed a boy by the front of his sweater and looked him in the eyes. His dark eyes flashed, and his normally neat hair fell into his eyes. "Do anything like that again and you will regret it."

He dropped him in a heap on the floor and pointed at Professor Jones. "I have three sisters. In my house, men don't throw things at women!" He sat back down with a thud. The class was silent.

Professor Jones opened his book, turned a few pages, and cleared his throat. "I guess we'll get started."

I sighed with relief and opened my notebook. The others did the same. President Elliott had told me if Professor Jones treated me badly, I should let him know. The situation was getting worse but I decided to give it another few days.

————◆————

At dinner that night, the March 26, 1937, issue of *The Exponent* confirmed what Mabel had said at the Abernathys'. She read aloud at the table before we all started eating: "Amelia Back; Confidence Unshaken. 'Nothing has happened to change my attitude toward the original project. Instead, I feel better about the ship itself than I ever have. And I'm more eager than ever to fly it again. If all goes well, I hope the plane may be reconditioned in from 30 to 60 days.'"

Since the reports about Amelia's flight had stopped while her plane was being repaired, the girls no longer congregated in our room. We still left the door open during homework hours in case anyone wanted to look at the map. Every now and then a few girls wandered in and stood in front of it.

"One to two months to repair the plane," Joan said. "Do you think Amelia is getting nervous while she waits?"

"Why would she?" Faye asked. "It was just a mechanical problem."

"Don't you worry about Amelia," Mabel assured them. "As soon as the plane is ready, she'll be ready."

That's what the news reports said, but I wasn't so sure. I felt there was something about Howland Island that made Amelia nervous. A week later a short letter arrived from her.

Dear Ginny,

I'm spending most of my time at the Lockheed plant in Burbank, California. I feel better being with the plane while the repair work is done. Say hi to Mabel. George sends his best.

Affectionately, A

———⟨◦⟩———

As March turned into April, the weather continued to warm up. *April showers bring May flowers,* I said to myself, as we walked to class. The air smelled like spring, earthy with just a hint of sweetness. I wondered what was about to bloom here in Indiana. At home, the crocuses would be trying to push their way through the melting snow.

After dropping Mabel and the girls off at the Home Economics Building, I slowly continued on my own. I wasn't in a hurry to see what Professor Jones had in store for me.

He walked into class, dropped his books on the counter, rubbed his hands together, and said, "Good morning, gentlemen."

I sighed and wondered how he would turn the boys against me this morning.

"I had a meeting with President Elliott and I am officially retiring in June." His face was solemn and he lowered his head at the end of his announcement. I sighed again because I knew what was coming.

The boys shouted "No!" and "That's not fair!" and "Stay!" The noise level rose. I got ready to duck but a knock made everyone stop and look at the door.

Professor Abernathy poked his head in. "I wonder if I might borrow a piece of chalk?"

"Ah, of course...come in," Professor Jones replied. The boys sat down and faced the front.

Professor Abernathy walked in. "So sorry to interrupt."

"Not at all. I have some right here." Professor Jones bent behind the counter.

Professor Abernathy locked eyes with the troublemakers. He pointed one finger at them until Professor Jones began to stand up. Without breaking eye contact, he slowly lowered his hand.

"Here we are. I found half a box."

Professor Abernathy turned to him. "Are you sure you can spare this much?"

"Yes, yes. The year is almost over."

"So it is," Professor Abernathy replied. "Thanks very much." He turned toward the troublemakers one more time and walked out.

Silence.

No one moved.

I wondered how he did it. He was a small, elderly man with a quiet, polite manner. But no one acted up in front of him.

Professor Jones cleared his throat. He turned to the blackboard and began to write. The boys quietly opened their notebooks. I looked at my desk and took a few deep breaths. David had just defeated Goliath.

Before Professor Jones had a chance to rile the boys in the next class, there was another knock on the door. Professor Weeks poked his head in.

"May I borrow some ink? My well has gone dry."

"Ah...yes of course." Professor Jones looked surprised but he bent under the counter again. He stood up with a large bottle of ink and Professor Weeks held out his inkwell. Professor Jones filled it, while everyone sat silently throughout the process.

"Thanks so much." Professor Weeks screwed the top on and left. Professor Jones frowned, turned to the blackboard, and began to write. The boys did the same.

I realized someone had gone to President Elliott—or maybe to Professor Abernathy. One, or both, of them had set up a plan to manage Professor Jones. *If this keeps up,* I told myself, *I might just make it.*

———⊶◦⊷———

As classes continued into May, final exams crept closer. Mabel, the boys, and I returned to our previous routine. We studied in the library and took breaks in the Union Building. Instead of tea, coffee, and hot chocolate, we drank cold Coca Cola or root beer. Mabel and I wore cotton dresses again and the boys wore short-sleeved shirts.

One evening, while Matt and I walked back to the residence together, we talked about his graduation.

"I've decided to accept Cap's job offer as a flight instructor," he said, "at least until I decide what I want to do next."

I stopped and gave him a hug. "I'm so glad you're not leaving!"

"So am I." He looked down at me and touched my cheek.

We linked arms and continued walking. I kept thinking about how relieved I felt when he said he was staying.

A sound off in the distance made me slow down and then stop. "Is that...music?" I asked.

"It's coming from the Union ballroom," Matt replied. "The band must be practicing for the Gala Week Dance." He took my hand and bowed. "May I have this dance?"

I looked around to make sure no one could see us. I curtsied and held out my arms. It took a few seconds for us to figure out where our hands went and then Matt took a tentative step sideways. I did the same and we stepped from side to side in time to the music.

"Hey, we're dancing!" Matt said. After two more songs, he stopped and looked down at me. He lifted my chin with his hand and gently pressed his lips against mine.

My heart pounded. This wasn't like a kiss on the forehead from Llewellyn. I felt warm and tingly all over. When Matt stood back, I opened my eyes and looked at him.

"That wasn't so bad," I said.

Matt laughed loudly. "I'm so relieved!"

"Me too," I replied. "I was nervous about what it would be like."

Matt held out his arm and I took it. We resumed our walk to the residence. It was time to write Llewellyn to tell him I was happy he'd found Edwina. I squeezed Matt's arm and he kissed the top of my head.

CHAPTER 29

NEW ROUTE

————◄○►————

A FEW DAYS later, another letter arrived from Amelia. Mabel and I read it sitting side by side on my bed.

Dear Ginny,

I have to change my plans. Instead of flying east to west, I'll fly west to east. Two months have passed since my first attempt. It's now monsoon season in Asia and the Pacific. Flying through monsoon rains is very dangerous. The muddy fields would make takeoffs almost impossible.

I'll leave from California but my first stop will be Miami, Florida. Harry Manning can't come along as advisor/navigator this time. He has to return to work before Fred and I leave. George is making arrangements for my new route.

As ever, A

Mabel posted the letter next to the map and she and I looked at the new route. I noticed Amelia's second-last stop was Howland Island and this time there would only be two pairs of eyes to find that tiny dot in the Pacific Ocean.

———◦———

In Professor Jones's next class, Professor Stewart popped in to borrow some engine oil. In the last class, Professor Ashworth asked to borrow paper. Then the semester ended.

Professor Jones closed his notebook and cleared his throat.

"Gentlemen, it has been a pleasure teaching you." His eyes scanned the class but carefully avoided mine. "I wish you the best of luck in the future. Although I'm retiring, I'll still be available if you ever need help."

The boys jumped to their feet and someone shouted, "Hip, hip, hooray." The others added their voices to the next two hoorays and then they crowded around the front counter to shake his hand.

I sat silently, in a numbed state. *It's over*, I told myself. *You made it. You finished first-year engineering.*

Then I thought of Mabel. She'd been right about Uncle Malcolm. His students did like and respect him. I might have felt sorry about his leaving but for the girls who would come after me. They wouldn't have to endure what I'd just been through. My shoulders started to relax as the reality set in.

The boys slowly packed up their books and walked out of class. Not one soul looked at me. When the room was empty, Jack and Jamie rushed back to my desk.

"Congratulations!" Jack grabbed my hand and shook it vigorously.

"Come on." Jamie pulled me to my feet. "We have to get to the coffee shop to tell the others."

"I'm in," Jack said. "I can always use a root beer!"

We packed up our books and walked up the centre aisle. Before we left, I paused and took one last look around before I closed the door behind me.

————◦◦————

Now that classes were over, it was exam time again. Our lives revolved around studying and for me the pressure was on. I had to prove my first-place standing at the end of last semester wasn't a fluke. As well as studying at the library with Mabel and the boys, I found myself carrying my notes wherever I went—the dining room, the laundry room, the coffee shop. I didn't notice the dark circles under my eyes, but Mabel did.

"Just let me put a bit of powder on your face." We stood in front of the mirror over my dresser. "People are going to think you're dying!"

When we weren't studying, we obsessively followed the news about Amelia's flights. She left Miami, Florida, early on the morning of June 1. *The Exponent* picked up her story on June 2. Mabel and I sat in the spring sunshine on the front steps of the residence. Each of us held one side of the newspaper and read silently: "We left the Miami International Airport at 5:56 AM (EST) today. For 13 minutes we climbed slowly, swinging southerly on our course toward Puerto Rico."

A second report, by W. F. O'Reilly of the *New York Herald Tribune*, described Amelia's journey into San Juan, Puerto Rico. "The 1,033 miles took 7 hours and 34 minutes to complete."

When she finished reading, Mabel turned to me. "Are the reports a day after her flights?"

"If they're in print, they are. Either Amelia or one of the assigned reporters has to telegraph the story to the newspaper. The flight is on one day, and the report is on the next."

"Well, so far, so good," Mabel said.

"This is the easy part," I replied. "The hard part comes later when they have to find less well known stops."

"I suppose you're right." Mabel folded the newspaper and picked up her books. "Let's go. The boys are waiting for us at the library. We can update our map later."

When we returned to our room, Mabel added a black line from Miami, Florida, to San Juan, Puerto Rico. We had decided black showed up best on our coloured map.

———◄◦►———

On June 3, the headline in *The Exponent* was "Amelia Hops to Caripito On Second Leg Of World Flight, by Amelia Earhart. Caripito, Venezuela, June 2."

Jamie read: "I rolled out of bed at 3:45 this morning in order to make a dawn take-off from San Juan, Puerto Rico, but aviation plans are as likely as those of mice and men to go astray, and it turned out the Electra did not lift her wheels from the runway until 5:40 A.M. Eastern Standard Time.

"I had intended to hop 1,000 miles direct to Paramaribo, Dutch Guiana, but owing to the later start and the fact that construction work at the San Juan airfield shortened the available takeoff distance, I decided to make Caripito for refueling purposes."

Barb, Joan, and Faye were waiting at our door when we returned from the coffee shop. "We read Amelia's in Caripito, Venezuela," Joan said. "We'd like to see where it is."

We walked into the room together and straight to the map. "You three look for Caripito and I'll get my black crayon," Mabel said. After some minutes, we found it and Mabel added the new line.

"I can't believe we actually know the person who's creating these lines," Faye said.

The other girls agreed and then drifted back to their own rooms to study.

It was hard for Mabel, the boys, and me to concentrate on the exams with all the exciting reports coming in about Amelia's flight. It was especially hard for Matt, who was in the same boat as me.

"I know I have a job with Cap when I graduate," he said, "but I have to prove I deserve it. I don't want people to think I'm getting a free ride just because I know him."

We agreed to read *The Exponent* only after we'd finished studying. At the coffee shop we were able to get drinks and copies of the newspaper. Matt opened the paper for Saturday, June 5 and spread it on the table.

"I'll read," Mabel said.

AMELIA FLIES OVER 960 MILES OF JUNGLE TO FORTALEZA
By Amelia Earhart.
Fortaleza, Brazil, June 4.

The weather at Paramaribo was perfect this morning, except for a morning mist from the Surinam River, when we took off, to skim the tree tops and then pull up.

Speaking of trees makes me realize we flew over 960 miles of jungle today. This, added to water hops totalling 370 miles, made a long but interesting day. I was very glad to see Fortaleza sitting just where it should be, according to the map, between the mountain and the sea, a beautiful spot.

We start tomorrow for Natal, Brazil—not so early as usual, although the habit of rising at 3 A.M. or thereabouts is becoming ingrained. Natal is only 267 miles away. There we plan to prepare for the South Atlantic hop (Natal to Dakar in French West Africa, 1,870 miles).

—◇—

The last exam ended on June 8. Mabel, Matt, Jamie, and I had all done such good work at Christmas, we were offered summer jobs in Lafayette: Mabel at the library, Matt and Jamie at the dairy barns, and me at the Abernathys' home. Mildred wanted to spend more time in Alabama with her mother. She'd improved since Christmas but she still needed help.

When I got back to the residence, Mabel wasn't there. I smiled when I thought about the home economics girls celebrating the end of the school year. A celebration for them was a trip to the fabric and notions shop in Lafayette.

While I waited for Mabel, I decided to write home to confirm I was staying here for the summer. In my mind I always knew this would be the case, but Mom and I hadn't discussed it at length before I left. With a paper and pen in front of me, I briefly held her hanky to my nose before I began.

Dear Mom, Nana, and Billy,

I hope this letter finds all of you well and happy. I just finished my final exams and I think I did well. I wish I could tell you I'll be coming home soon but I can't.

You may remember me telling you about the Abernathys, the lovely people I worked for at Christmas. They have offered me a summer job and I've agreed to stay in West Lafayette. I would love to be in Harbour Grace with all of you, jigging for cod, picking blueberries, and eating fish and brewis. You'll never know how much I miss the sound of the sheets snapping in the wind when Nana hangs them in the backyard.

How are Aunt Rose and Uncle Harry? Is he still as smitten by Miss Rorke as he was last summer? Uncle Harry wearing aftershave lotion! Did you ever believe you would see that day? And how is Billy doing? Still working for Aunt Rose at the hotel, I hope. And what about Dad? Is he still in Toronto?

As much as I long to be back in Harbour Grace, the truth is I need my salary—not just to send money home but to use while I'm here. My scholarship covers my tuition, books, and residence, but I still need money for anything else. I hope you understand.

I'll enclose another money order and get this in the mail. I love you all and miss you so much.

Ginny

After I mailed my letter, I joined everyone at the coffee shop. June 8 found Amelia and Fred Noonan in Africa—Dakar to be exact. Since exams were over, we would be able to follow Amelia whenever we weren't working.

Back in our room, Mabel added Paramaribo, Dutch Guiana; Fortaleza, Brazil; Natal, Brazil; and Dakar, French West Africa, to our map. She had to use a ruler to draw the long line across the Atlantic Ocean from South America to Africa.

When *The Exponent* had no news about Amelia, we went to the library to read the *New York Herald Tribune*. We sat around a table with the newspaper in front of us, while Mabel read.

"'June 10, 1937, Dakar—We took three days here to have the engines checked. Then we made the long, hot journey across Africa with stops at Gao, Fort-Lamy, El Fasher, Khartoum, and Massawa. Fred found navigation difficult because the few maps available are often inaccurate.

We continued to Eritrea and then nonstop to Karachi, Pakistan—an aviation first, as no one has previously flown from the Red Sea to India.'"

"She must be halfway home by now," Jamie said.

"Let me add these new stops to our map and I'll let you know," Mabel replied.

◦

There hadn't been any reports while Amelia and Fred crossed Africa. The stops were probably too isolated to allow for easy communication. It was June 17 before the next installment appeared in *The Exponent*.

We decided to meet in one of the date rooms at the Women's Residence, for a change of scenery. Ed and Jack were busy so there were only the four of us. Jamie spread the paper out on the coffee table but before we started reading, Mabel gave an update.

"I've checked the map; Amelia and Fred are halfway home."

"How long do you think it will be before they're back in the United States?" I asked.

"At the rate they're going, I'd say early July," Matt replied.

I couldn't wait to see Amelia and ask her to fill in the details of her flight that weren't covered in the newspaper reports. The trip sounded like it was going smoothly but I knew there was probably much more to the story.

"Whose turn is it to read?" I asked.

"I think it's mine," Jamie said. He read:

Calcutta, India, June 17, 1937.

We reached Calcutta today. We've made 15 stops thus far. The aircraft has performed well, and there have been no major problems. The next legs are to Rangoon, Bangkok, Singapore, and Java. We expect to be in Java by June 24.

"Amelia must be getting tired," I said.

"And the heat must be bad in that part of the world," Matt added.

"Don't worry about Amelia," Mabel said. "She's used to long-distance flying."

I agreed. If anyone could do it, it was Amelia.

———◦———

On June 25, *The Exponent* carried an update. As usual, we met at the coffee shop and Ed read.

AMELIA SAFE IN JAVA; EXPECTED HERE JULY 2.

Sourabaya, June 25, 1937.

Amelia Earhart landed here today en route to Kupang, Timor Island, on her round the world flight. She plans to remain here until tomorrow.

Miss Earhart intends to start her 1,200-mile hop to Kupang tomorrow. From Kupang she will fly to Darwin, Australia.

Dr. Elliott said Tuesday during an NBC broadcast that he had recently been in communication with Miss Earhart, and that she had assured him unless an unseen mishap overtakes her, she will be able to appear on the Policy and Technology Institute program here July 2.

"That's only a week from today!" Mabel exclaimed.
"Will we need tickets?" Jamie asked.
"I'll check with Cap," Matt offered. "He should know."
I sat quietly, but my heart was pounding.
One more week.

CHAPTER 30

HOWLAND ISLAND

———◄○►———

THE BOYS WERE working late when the next edition of *The Exponent* came out on June 29. Mabel and I read it on the front steps before dinner.

AMELIA STARTS ON HOP TO NEW GUINEA FROM AUSTRALIA.

Port Darwin, Australia, June 28, 1937.

Amelia Earhart Putnam left here at 3 P.M. (CST) today on her 1,500-mile hop to Lae, New Guinea. Miss Earhart flew here from the Dutch East Indies. She expects to fly to Howland Island from Lae.

Miss Earhart, flying an $80,000 silver monoplane purchased by the Purdue Research Foundation, is on her second attempt to fly around the world, having cracked-up at Honolulu on her first effort.

"I wish they hadn't mentioned her crash," I said. "It feels like a bad omen."

"Don't worry," Mabel replied. "Amelia has everything under control."

We folded the paper and joined the girls going into the dining room. Most of the conversation was about Amelia's flight but a few girls wanted to talk about exams. Mabel answered a number of questions the others couldn't figure out. Although Mabel had great fashion sense, I hadn't realized what an expert she was in the other subjects. I suppose I'd been so focused on my own situation, I hadn't paid enough attention to what Mabel was accomplishing.

The next day, we were all back in the library. We sat around one of the large tables for the next report in the *New York Herald Tribune*:

Lae, New Guinea, June 29, 1937.

They reached Lae, New Guinea, after a 1,200 mile flight in 7 and 3/4 hours.

The engines were thoroughly checked, the spark plugs cleaned, and the fuel pump and the autopilot repaired. Everything not needed for the transpacific flight, including parachutes and some survival equipment, was packed to be sent home. Earhart cabled the last of her articles to the *New York Herald Tribune*. She then met with senior government officials and took care of details such as fumigation of the plane, a check of immunization certificates, and customs clearance.

There are reports that Noonan and Earhart were exhausted at that point, causing a delay in their take off for Howland, 2,227 nautical miles from Lae. Meanwhile, the US Coast Guard Cutter *Itasca* is waiting off Howland to act as a radio contact. The Navy has a weather officer and two mechanics waiting on the island with a run-in cylinder assembly, new spark plugs, oil, gas, and food.

A seaplane tender, USS *Swan*, is approximately 200 miles northeast of the island to monitor the Howland/Hawaii leg. Other ships—USS *Ontario* and USS *Myrtle Bank*—are positioned along the intended flight track between the Nukumanu Islands and Howland Island."

Two details in the newspaper account added to my nervousness about this leg of the trip. Noonan and Earhart were exhausted and the Navy support showed how concerned everyone was about finding that tiny island. All I could do was believe in Amelia the way she had always believed in me.

———◦———

The next night, Mabel, Matt, Jamie, Jack, Ed, the senior Elliotts and I met at the Abernathys' home at seven o'clock. We wanted to hear the first reports of Amelia's landing on their radio. According to a cable from Howland Island earlier in the day, Amelia and Fred left Lae on July 1, at ten o'clock local time. The weather forecast was favourable: headwinds of 12–15 knots, partly cloudy conditions with rain squalls, and visibility that was mostly unlimited.

By eight, I was jumping up to pass tea and cookies every few minutes. When I wasn't doing that, I sat twisting my napkin and trying not to babble. Professor Abernathy turned the radio dial from station to station but none had news.

Finally, through a burst of static, we heard, "No contact with Amelia since 20:14 GMT."

I jumped up. "But that means they've been in the air for twenty hours and fourteen minutes." I looked around at their faces, but they didn't understand what I was getting at. "They only have fuel for a twenty-one-hour flight!"

"Just wait," Professor Abernathy said calmly. "She'll land in exactly forty-six minutes." He smiled and nodded and the others did the same.

I sat down and continued twisting my napkin. Everyone remained silent while Professor Abernathy turned the dial again. Forty-six minutes passed with no news.

I paced between the living room and kitchen.

Eventually a voice cut through the static. It was the Coast Guard Headquarters in San Francisco. I stopped pacing and the others leaned out of their chairs.

"This message received from Captain Thompson on the *Itasca*: Proceeding north at full speed."

I stood stock-still. There was only one reason for the *Itasca* to speed north.

Amelia was down.

Mabel stood up and put her hand on my shoulder. "She'll be fine, Ginny. No one knows flying like Amelia."

"We'll sit here as long as it takes to find out she's safe," Mrs. Abernathy added.

I stared at a point on the opposite wall. Then I turned away from Mabel, walked through the kitchen, and out the back door. On the porch, I took deep breaths and raised my face to the sky. It was dark and a heavy bank of clouds hid the moon.

◦

When I awoke, the sky was getting light. I was huddled in a big blanket on the back porch. Mrs. Abernathy sat across from me in her wheelchair. "I sent the others home because I knew you needed some time alone."

The memories from last night hit me like a speeding train. My breath came in gulps and tears rolled down my face. For a long time, I sat crying. When I was able to drag myself to my feet, Mrs. Abernathy took my hand and led me inside to the sofa.

With my head on her lap, the sounds in the house faded and I found myself in a long hallway. At the end was a small room with a single chair. I sat down. Suddenly the floor collapsed and I fell into blackness. The wind whistled in my ears, my eyes watered, and a bone-deep cold surrounded me. The sound of screaming filled my ears. My head jerked to one side and my eyes stung—but at least the screaming stopped. Through my tears, I saw Mrs. Abernathy and I knew I was safe.

But what did the dream mean? Why was I falling through blackness into such cold?

I turned and looked at Mrs. Abernathy. "You're all right now," she said. "Just a whiff of smelling salts to calm you down." She handed a small bottle to Professor Abernathy. "I think a glass of warm milk might help too."

A few minutes later, he returned and Mrs. Abernathy helped me sit up. She slowly lifted a glass to my lips and I swallowed. It tasted horrible but I finished it. I lay down and Mrs. Abernathy covered me with a quilt.

"You're safe now," she soothed. "Relax and sleep."

The next time I opened my eyes, the room was dark. Matt sat in the chair beside the sofa. I saw his face in the dim light shining in from the hall. "I feel like I'm floating," I said.

"Professor Abernathy gave you a shot of brandy."

"No wonder the milk tasted so bad."

Matt smiled. "Go back to sleep. I'll be right here."

———◄○►———

I bolted upright and didn't know where I was. Matt put his arms around me and called the Abernathys. When Mrs. Abernathy arrived, she sat where Matt had been and put her arms around me.

"She's shaking like a leaf, Charles. The hot water bottle is in the closet in the bathroom."

When he returned, Mrs. Abernathy wrapped it in a blanket. She eased me onto my side and placed the warmth behind my back. The shaking slowly stopped and my body relaxed.

In the afternoon, Mabel joined Matt and the Abernathys. "The USS *Lexington* has joined the *Itasca* and the *Swan* in the search for Amelia," she said. "And a PBY flying boat has been dispatched from Hawaii."

I slowly turned my head away from them and looked at the ceiling.

"Amelia is dead," I replied.

No one said a word.

CHAPTER 31

RECOVERY

———◆◇◆———

OVER THE NEXT few days, the Abernathys encouraged me to talk. I made an effort to tell them what they wanted to hear because I knew they were trying to help. What I couldn't tell them was how I really felt—like an empty shell where a girl named Ginny had once lived.

Mabel brought fresh clothes and I moved into the Abernathys' spare bedroom. I felt safe there and had no real desire to leave until Mrs. Abernathy expressed a different idea.

"It's time to get you out of your nightgown and into the fresh air."

When I was dressed, she sent me out to the front porch. A few minutes later, she pushed the screen door open with her hip. I stood up and took one of the glasses of lemonade she offered before we both sat down.

"I have a couple of telegrams for you to read," she said. "They arrived the day after...a few days ago. I opened them because I wanted to make sure there wasn't an emergency at home. Read your mom's first."

DEAR GINNY PLEASE COME HOME STOP I DON'T WANT TO LOSE YOU TOO STOP LOVE MOM

I laid it on my lap and looked at Mrs. Abernathy.

"Don't worry," she said. "I answered it as if I was you. I said I was in shock and had to think about what to do next. I signed your name."

"Good. Thank you."

I opened the second one.

SORRY ABOUT AMELIA STOP FOLLOW YOUR DREAM STOP NOTHING HERE FOR YOU STOP LOVE UNCLE HARRY

I put the telegrams back in their envelopes. Tears flowed down my face. "I don't know what to do," I whispered.

"What are your options?" Mrs. Abernathy asked.

"I can stay here and go back to school in September...or I can go home."

"What can you do at home?"

"That's a good question. I've never been a typical girl. I always preferred engines to cooking or sewing. Just ask my mother. I was a complete failure in her eyes until I finally convinced her I could be a pilot."

Mrs. Abernathy smiled and sat quietly, her hands folded in her lap. Some time passed before I spoke again.

"If I can't fly, what else can I do?"

I took the hanky with the embroidered blue flowers out of my pocket and dried my eyes. The faintest scent of lavender lingered.

"I know my mother is worried but Uncle Harry is right. There's nothing there for me. If I want to help them, I have to learn how to fly."

"I was hoping you'd say that. I'll give you directions to the telegraph office," Mrs. Abernathy said.

We sat silently for some time before I stood and picked up the lemonade glasses. "I'd better get back into the kitchen. Mildred will think I've gone on strike!"

Mrs. Abernathy smiled. "She hasn't said a word but she'll probably be happy to be on her way home."

————◄○►————

The next morning, Mildred left for Alabama and I started working alone. I stood in the kitchen preparing breakfast. It was exactly what I needed, activity for my body and rest for my mind.

I ate with the Abernathys at the dining room table and told them about my plans for supper. "It was too hot to use the oven yesterday so I roasted a chicken last night while Mildred packed. I also made a tomato aspic and boiled potatoes and eggs for potato salad."

Both of them made complimentary remarks and Professor Abernathy even rubbed his hands together in anticipation.

Cooking for these kind people made the hole in my heart a little less painful.

Next to the Abernathys, Matt spent the most time with me. He came over after dinner and we sat on the back porch steps. Matt put his arm around my shoulders and we talked. Having him close gave me a feeling of calm.

No matter how hard I tried to distract myself with housework, one question kept coming back. What had gone wrong? I knew Amelia's habits. She always planned to the smallest detail.

But then there was Howland Island—that tiny dot in the Pacific Ocean. Amelia had always seemed nervous about finding it. On her first attempt, she'd taken Harry Manning as a third pair of eyes. She should have been confident that the three of them could find it, but then she ground looped taking off from Hawaii. I always wondered if that was caused by a mechanical problem, as she claimed, or if she had been nervous and made an error.

On her second attempt, Harry couldn't join them. He had to return to work. Did this cause Amelia more concern about finding Howland Island?

One night, Matt asked me about Amelia. "Why were you so sure she was dead, even before the search was called off?"

I hadn't spoken to anyone about that yet. I didn't want them to think I was delirious.

"When the radio announcer said the *Itasca* was steaming north, I thought I heard Amelia's voice," I said, avoiding Matt's eye. "She was shouting Fred's name. At that moment all the air seemed to leave the living room and I had to get out." I looked at Matt and crossed my arms over my chest. "Then I saw her, the night you were sitting beside the sofa."

"Is that why you sat up so suddenly and couldn't remember where you were?"

I started trembling and Matt put his arm around my shoulders. "The plane was nose-down in the water," I whispered. My eyes filled with tears. "Amelia was climbing over the gas tank behind her seat. It looked as if she was trying to get to Fred. Maybe he was injured." I cleared my throat and continued. "Before she could reach him, the nose dropped lower and the plane slid under the waves."

Matt kissed the tears off my cheeks and pulled me closer. He didn't say anything. I wrapped my arms around him and sank into his warmth.

We sat like that for a long time.

CHAPTER 32

MOVING ON

————◀○▶————

I T WAS THE end of August, and Mabel and I leaned on the windowsill in our room to watch the new girls arriving. They came in cars and taxis, which meant it was the afternoon.

"At least they don't have to carry their luggage very far," I said.

Mabel chuckled at the memory. "Did we look that scared?"

"I did, but you were cool and calm," I replied. "I was convinced I was never getting off that railway platform until you arrived."

"You definitely looked like a fish out of water!"

"You're turning into a Newfoundlander right in front of my eyes!"

We both laughed and stood up just as the bell rang for afternoon tea. Our friends from the second floor—Barb, Joan, Faye, Elizabeth, Sarah, and Joanne—sat in the dining room with some of the new girls. After the introductions, we talked about what we'd done all summer.

In a pause in the conversation, Joanne looked at me.

"We were so sorry to hear about Amelia. But it's only been two months! They could still find her."

"She's—" I was going to say "dead," but a piece of sandwich stuck in my throat. I took a sip of tea.

"I'm hoping they find her on one of those deserted islands," Elizabeth said. "Some of them have fresh water." She looked at the others and they nodded.

"I heard she was captured by the Japanese," Barb added. "Maybe they'll release her and she'll come home."

I glanced at Mabel. It was probably best I hadn't said Amelia was dead. My friends were trying to console me.

"There's a new movie at The Luna!" Faye said, changing the subject. "Let's all go after dinner."

"That sounds like fun!" Joan replied. She looked at me expectantly.

It did sound like fun but there was something about the movies that bothered me. "Maybe next time," I said.

"Sure," Sarah said. "We'll let you know what it was like."

We walked up the stairs to the second floor together and the stories about what the girls did over the summer continued. I couldn't get into the spirit. The world seemed grey these days. I had decided to stay at Purdue and get my pilot's licence, but the adventure was gone, Amelia was gone, and the joy was gone.

Mabel kept looking at me, and when I caught her eye she smiled and linked arms with me. At our door, we said goodbye and told the others we would see them at dinner.

Mabel and I sat at our desks, checking our class schedules. When I put mine down, she asked if she could look at it.

"Applied Mathematics! Ugh, I'll stick to my Applied Fashion Design, thank you very much."

"But I start my flying lessons," I countered. "I bet you'd like to do that."

"Thanks, but no thanks. The North Atlantic is not for me."

I smiled and turned my chair to face her. "It's not the movie I don't want to see. It's the newsreel." I paused. "I'm not ready to see Amelia's face and hear her voice."

Mabel reached for my hand. "I forgot about the newsreels. They're probably full of theories about where she might be."

"That's why I don't read the newspapers or listen to the radio."

"That makes sense. Maybe in a few more weeks."

I smiled and nodded. Mabel patted my hand and we went back to our schedules.

Two days later, Mabel and I walked to our first class of second year. The sun warmed our faces, the birds sang, and a gentle breeze ruffled our hair. It was hard to believe the world could be so beautiful without Amelia in it.

"Guess what I heard at breakfast?" Mabel asked. "Apparently Uncle Malcolm didn't retire. He was asked to leave."

My eyes widened. "Really?"

"And there's more. President Elliott allowed him to stay on staff but only working part-time with the graduate students. At the moment they're all male."

"Female grad students will catch up with him sooner or later."

"But they're safe for now!" she replied.

I nodded. Mabel's uncle Malcolm had almost destroyed our friendship, but we were on the same page now.

We said goodbye at the Home Economics Building and walked in opposite directions. I thought about Professor Jones and actually felt sorry for him. I knew he couldn't stop the winds of change that were blowing toward him and I doubted that he could adapt. As Nana used to say: "The branch that can't bend with the wind will break."

At the Mechanical Engineering Building, there were a few boys filing in but no one harassed me. I opened the door and the familiar smell of fresh wax welcomed me. Before I got halfway down the hall, Jamie and Jack walked in.

"Ready for a calmer year?" Jack asked.

I gave him a hug and said, "You can't even imagine how ready I am."

We sat in the front seats for a few minutes before Professor Osborne arrived. He was younger than most engineering profs at Purdue—tall and slim with brown hair and big brown eyes. Instead of a suit and tie, he wore an open-neck shirt and sweater. The first thing he said was, "Miss Ross, gentlemen, welcome back."

CHAPTER 33

GROUND SCHOOL

OUR NEXT CLASS was at the airport: the first day of ground school. As I walked along the road with Jack and Jamie, voices floated from the cornfields beyond the trees. I remember what Mabel told me this time last year and concluded the harvest must have begun.

Before long, we saw the Purdue University Airport sign. I slowed down and wrung my hands. Memories flooded my mind—Amelia, the Electra, her mechanic, Bo McKneely, and the promise of an around-the-world flight. The boys must have noticed my hesitation because they each held out an elbow.

"Come on, Ginny Ross from Harbour Grace, Newfoundland," Jamie said. "This is the fun part of engineering!"

I grabbed Jamie's arm and then reached for Jack's. We walked this way until we got to the tarmac in front of the hangar. Cap stood next to a Taylor Cub and shook hands with each student as he arrived. I got a hug and Cap whispered in my ear, "I'm so sorry about Amelia. I miss her every time I look at the spot where the Electra sat." He patted my back before he let me go.

I brushed a tear off my cheek and whispered, "Me too," before I stepped back next to Jamie and Jack. We chatted in the warm sun until the rest of the class arrived. Ten of us had signed up for the lessons.

Matt walked out of the hangar and winked at me. Then he stood next to Cap and assumed a serious expression.

"I'd like you to meet my assistant, Matt Baker," Cap said. "Some of you may already know him as Jamie's older brother, but here he is an instructor. His word is my word and it's law. I know you'll show him the same respect you've always shown me."

We all smiled at Matt and nodded.

"Now, allow me to introduce your new best friend." Cap swept his arm over the small plane and we all clapped. We longed to get into the sky but knew that we had to pass ground school first.

Cap led us into a classroom located inside the hangar. It looked much like a regular classroom—a long counter at the front with a blackboard behind and tables and chairs in front. The big difference was the wall of windows that looked into the hangar. If Cap was teaching in here, he could still see what was going on out there.

I sat in the front row with Jamie on one side and Jack on the other. My twin brothers: blond-haired, carefree Jamie and dark-haired, protective Jack. I couldn't have asked for better friends.

Cap walked to the front and waited for silence. "Time to get down to work so we can get you into the sky."

We all clapped until he held up his hands. With a big smile, he said, "The first thing you have to do is stop clapping every time I mention flying. The second is, write down whatever I put on this blackboard."

Our response was the sound of rustling papers and whispered voices, followed by silence as we wrote: *Ground School Course Outline. Topic 1: Aircraft Terminology.*

"Just as you did in your small engines class last year, I'll introduce the theory in here and then you'll apply it to a plane in the hangar. This is a list of aircraft terminology—essentially, the parts of a plane and their function. Fill them in as well as you can and Matt will help you with the ones you don't know."

I knew most of the terms from of my lessons with Uncle Harry. Jamie leaned over and looked at my answers.

"What the heck is a port stabilizer?" he whispered.

"It's the horizontal part of the tail. Because it's on the left, it's the *port* stabilizer."

"So the one on the right is the starboard stabilizer?"

I smiled and gave him a thumbs-up. While the others continued writing, my eyes wandered into the hangar to where the Electra had stood. My heart pounded, but with a few deep breaths, slowly returned to a regular rhythm. Amelia was gone but the pain was easing.

Matt brought our attention back to the front of the class to hear our answers. He wrote the ones that most people missed on the blackboard. Then we went into the hangar and identified each of the parts on a Taylor Cub.

I couldn't believe the lesson was over so quickly. We thanked Cap and Matt and headed back to the residence.

Over the next weeks and months we covered: Instruments; Federal Aviation Regulations; Aeronautical Decision Making; Airport Operation; Weather Theory; Aircraft Performance; Weight and Balance; and Navigation. The "fun part of engineering" was creeping back into my life.

———◦———

Ground school made the fall and winter pass quickly. It was the spring of 1938 and I finally felt comfortable enough to go to a movie with Matt. He held my hand as we walked to the Luna Theater. *Night Must Fall* starring Robert Montgomery and Rosalind Russell was playing. Behind us, Jamie and Mabel also held hands.

"I heard this is a thriller," Mabel said.

"Jack saw it last week," Jamie replied. "He said it's a good movie—and Amelia wasn't mentioned in the newsreels."

I took a deep breath and felt my body relax. Matt bought our tickets and we joined the line at the concession stand.

"What would you like?" Matt asked.

"Popcorn, please." I closed my eyes and breathed in the smell of melted butter.

I barely had time to thank him before the lights flickered to tell us the movie was starting. We hurried to our seats just as a swell of music was followed by a title on the screen. A man announced, "The News Parade" and all the lights went out.

"EUROPE'S ZERO HOUR," the headline came on the screen at the same time as the announcer read it. Then we saw a small man with a funny mustache, shouting into a microphone. A huge crowd of people responded with cheers and raised arms in some kind of salute.

The announcer continued to speak as the images changed. "The Chancellor of Germany, Adolf Hitler, demands self-determination for all Germans living in Austria and Czechoslovakia. Nazis living in Austria have rioted and invited Hitler to invade."

The events in Europe had finally pushed Amelia's disappearance off the newsreels.

———⟨◦⟩———

We emerged into the cool evening air and started walking toward the coffee shop.

"Jack was right," Mabel said. "That was a good movie—and there was nothing about Amelia in the newsreel."

"But who would have thought such a funny-looking little man as Adolf Hitler could replace Amelia Earhart in the newsreels," Jamie replied.

"Do you think he's as dangerous as he sounds?" I asked.

"You saw the crowds at his rallies," Matt replied. "I think the countries around Germany will be keeping a sharp eye on him."

"So they should," Jamie agreed.

CHAPTER 34

FLIGHT

B EFORE WE KNEW it, the summer had passed and we were back in class. The newsreels brought an answer to the question we had been asking each other all summer: "Can anyone stop Adolf Hitler?"

We watched the screen as Neville Chamberlain, the prime minister of Great Britain, stood in the doorway of an airplane and waved a peace agreement signed by Hitler. The crowd cheered and waved back.

After the movie, Matt held the door to the theatre open and we filed out.

"Do you think that agreement will stop Hitler?" I asked the group.

"Chamberlain seemed to think so," Mabel replied.

"As long as you don't live in a country that was given to Hitler to keep him happy, I suppose the peace treaty might work," Jack said.

"I can't see him being happy with just the Sudetenland," said Matt. "I've got a feeling this is just the beginning."

———⊲◦▻———

A week later we crowded around Cap Aretz in the hangar. "Welcome back," he said. "I'm pleased to see all ten of you back. Now on to the best part of training for your pilot's license—the flying!"

He let the cheering die down before he continued. "Because I only allow two planes in the air at once, you can stay here to watch or come back when it's your turn." He passed a sheet of paper to each of us with the schedule for our time in the air. "Some of you won't go up until this afternoon."

Bill Troost and I were first on the schedule.

"I know this hasn't been done much in the hallowed halls of Purdue University," Cap said, "but around here it's ladies first."

Cap was listed as my instructor and Matt was listed as Bill's. The other eight students decided to observe the takeoffs and landings until it was their turn.

My heart pounded as Cap and I walked toward our plane. It pounded harder when I stepped over the low door and sat down. The familiar smell of leather and engine oil surrounded me.

Jamie turned the propeller, the engine roared, and we taxied to the runway. Cap shouted every step as he carried it out. He pushed the throttle forward, gained speed, and bounced down the runway. My stomach lurched when the ground fell away and we lifted into the air.

The sun shone brightly in a clear blue sky. The trees were beginning to change colour, and splashes of red and yellow dotted the landscape. The vibration of the engine, the roar of the wind, and the view of the campus brought Amelia back.

Cap was talking, but I was no longer with him.

I was at Aunt Rose's hotel with Amelia, just before she left for the airstrip. She had just finished telling me about her next project: attracting more women into aviation. She and her husband, George, were looking for a university to partner with.

"Girls could take academic subjects and flying lessons at the same time," she explained. "That way they could graduate with a university degree and a pilot's license. Just think of what that could do for bright girls like you!"

And look at what it had done for me. It was a beautiful day and I was flying. In spite of the bumpy road to get here, my dream had come true.

It was at that moment I realized I hadn't lost Amelia. She was sitting right here beside me, pointing out all the landmarks that were so much more familiar to me than they'd been on my first flight with Cap—Ross Ade Stadium, the Armory, the Memorial Gymnasium, and the Union Building.

A peaceful feeling washed over me. My hands unclenched and my breathing became regular. My shoulders relaxed and I sank into the leather seat. I felt as if I'd come home after a long trip.

"Ginny, you there?" Cap's voice brought me back into the plane. "Time to go home," he said. "Watch what I'm doing."

"Aye, aye, Captain." I leaned forward and looked over his shoulder. It was time to concentrate on the future.

Cap touched down and taxied back to the hangar. He stopped the engine and we stepped out. Before we joined the other students, he turned and looked at me. "It must be hard to fly without thinking about Amelia."

"Was it that obvious?"

"It's just a matter of time. You'll see." He draped his arm around my shoulders and we walked toward the hangar.

———◄○►———

Flying lessons and watching the newsreels at the movies became our group's new routine that fall. As it turned out, Matt had been right about Hitler. He ignored the peace agreement and began invading neighbouring countries.

"Where is Czechoslovakia?" Mabel asked as we walked out of The Luna one afternoon. The newsreel had shown Nazi troops crossing the border.

"Next to Germany, but I'd have to check it on a map," Matt said.

"Professor Abernathy has a big atlas on the bookshelf in his living room," I said. I'd dusted it enough times but never looked inside. "We could consult that."

"Then let's go," Jamie said. "They usually like company."

Mrs. Abernathy was delighted to see us and put on the kettle for tea. Professor Abernathy took down the atlas and put it on the dining room table. We all leaned over until Matt pointed to Czechoslovakia.

"Wow. If he could just take a whole country that easily, where will he go next?" Mabel asked.

"Wherever he wants, unless something drastic happens to stop him," Professor Abernathy replied.

Nothing drastic happened, and Hitler invaded Poland. We walked into The Luna to see our weekly movie. The newsreel began with a swell of dramatic music and a voiceover from the announcer: "Poland, September 1939. The German foe begins its ruthless march of conquest." The music faded and the sound of heavy artillery took over. The theatre seemed to shake as the bombs landed.

"Towns and cities lie in ruins as the German army moves across Poland," the announcer continued. "People dig through the rubble that was once their homes, looking for missing family members. Fires are burning everywhere, and the sound of sirens fills the air."

I squeezed Matt's hand so tightly he looked at me and whispered, "Are you all right?"

"I can't believe this is happening," I whispered back. The theatre echoed with each firing of the huge guns.

"As food supplies run out, bread lines are formed, and women scrounge for food in farmers' fields," the announcer continued. "Our cameras caught the aftermath of German fighters strafing a potato field with machine guns. Seven women died in this attack."

The camera panned across the field showing the bodies. "The women know the Germans are firing on civilians but they can't let their families starve. This is the price they pay."

The camera zoomed in on one of the women and my hand flew up to my mouth. A small child sat crying beside her.

We walked out of the theatre in silence. I looked up into the clear blue sky and let the sun warm my face. I closed my eyes and saw another sky, filled with smoke, fire, and planes careening toward Earth. The gentle landscape of West Lafayette, with its cornfields and red brick buildings, sat in stark contrast to bombed-out buildings, collapsed walls, and rubble-filled streets. It didn't seem possible that one man could inflict so much pain and suffering on his fellow humans.

"How can he get away with this?" I asked no one in particular.

Mabel and Jamie just shook their heads.

"The problem is there's no one strong enough to stop him," Matt said.

Not knowing what else to do, we walked to the Abernathys' and looked at the atlas again.

"Czechoslovakia and now Poland," Jack said. "Who's next?"

Professor Abernathy confirmed what Matt had said. "That's hard to say. There's no country strong enough to stop Hitler. He's been secretly building up the German military to the point where no one can stand up to him and win."

The evening ended with Professor Abernathy giving us permission to plot Hitler's march across Europe in his atlas. "This is history," he said, "and we must document it."

Countries continued to fall like dominoes—Norway, Denmark, France, Belgium, Luxembourg, and the Netherlands.

One evening we were gathered at the Abernathys' listening to the bombing of Paris on the radio.

"Is it possible that Britain is next?" Matt asked.

"I never dreamed it would come to this," Professor Abernathy said, shaking his head. "But I'm afraid it looks like that's his next target.

CHAPTER 35

JUNE 1940

◄○►

Aₗₜₕₒᵤgₕ THERE WAS little to celebrate in Europe, in West Lafayette, there was a happy event: Mabel, Jamie, Jack, and I were graduating. Unlike Matt and Ed, who had wanted their graduation to be a quiet event, Mabel wanted a celebration. "After all, there are four of us," she said.

We stood in a line outside the Memorial Gymnasium, waiting for our class to be seated. My heart raced as I searched for Jack and Jamie. Because we had to sit in alphabetical order, I had Quentin Robinson on one side of me and Peter Roxton on the other. Quentin had always been polite in class but Peter was not a fan of mine. He kept giving me the evil eye as we inched closer to the front doors. He and many others still blamed me for the sudden retirement of Professor Jones.

When we entered the gymnasium, I gasped at the decorations. American flags hung vertically from the ceiling, along with bunting in red, white, and blue. Bleachers lined the side walls and the rest of the floor space was filled with chairs facing the stage—and what a stage it was! Plants and small trees surrounded it. Chairs lined the back wall and a lectern stood at centre stage. A set of stairs led up to it. I followed Quentin to the seats that had been reserved for us and sat down. Slowly the gymnasium filled with the families and friends of the graduates.

I sat quietly with my hands folded in my lap and closed my eyes. I saw Amelia standing at the lectern during her Convocation address in my freshman year. She smiled and waved as we applauded loudly. My pounding heart seemed to slow down and the sense of calm I felt on my flight with Cap returned. Amelia was here and she was smiling at me.

I thought of my family and friends in Harbour Grace, and in my mind's eye, they were here too. They sat in the front row with Amelia. Nana dabbed her eyes with her hanky; Mom chatted with Amelia on one side and Uncle Harry on the other. Dad and Billy each held one of Aunt Rose's hands, and Llew turned around and gave me a thumbs-up. I smiled back and gave him a little wave.

My eyes flew open when Quentin nudged me. The platform party was filing onto the stage. We all stood up and the band played the national anthem. When the music stopped, the people on the stage sat down in the row of chairs behind the lectern. President Elliott walked to the microphone and asked us to please be seated.

"Ladies and gentlemen, it is my pleasure to welcome you to the 1940 Purdue University Commencement. We will begin with aeronautical engineering and proceeded in alphabetical order through the other faculties."

We stood up and formed a line in the side aisle. I stood first in the class, but asked President Elliott not to mention it. Although he wanted to celebrate my success as a female engineering student, I was afraid of the Peter Roxtons in the audience. I knew I had earned my way onto that stage but I didn't need a disgruntled classmate reminding me of how hard the journey had been. President Elliott agreed that it was better to keep the ceremony positive.

When my name was called, I grasped the railing and walked up the stairs. My heart pounded so hard I could hear it in my ears. I shook hands with the man who had supported me from my first year at Purdue. When he placed the hood over my head and adjusted it on my shoulders, he whispered in my ear, "I'm so proud of you, Ginny."

I swallowed the lump in my throat. "Thank you...for *all* you've done," I whispered back.

He squeezed my shoulder and I walked across the stage with my head held high. Matt, Mabel, Ed, Mrs. Elliott, Miss Schleman, all our friends from the Women's Residence, the Bakers, the Andersons, and the Abernathys cheered wildly. Others in the crowd joined in...but not everyone. Many people still thought women did not belong in engineering.

—◆—

After the ceremony, we engulfed Mrs. Abernathy in our black robes when we bent over her wheelchair to hug her. She looked as if she was under attack from a family of ravens. Professor Abernathy shook our hands and invited us for afternoon tea. It was only fitting, since the Abernathys' house had become our second home.

When we left the gymnasium, Matt asked if he and I could walk alone. He had something to tell me. I looked up at him and smiled, but he didn't make eye contact.

I frowned. "What is it?"

He stopped and looked at me "I don't know how to tell you this."

I took his hand. "Just spit it all out at once."

He finally looked me in the eyes. "I'm joining the military. Professor Abernathy is right. England is Hitler's next target and President Roosevelt won't just sit back and let that happen."

"But the United States is neutral." My heart was pounding and my mouth felt dry.

"Roosevelt will find a way to get supplies over there...and he'll need pilots to do it."

"Then I'll join too."

Matt smiled sadly and squeezed my hand. "The Army Air Corps doesn't accept female pilots."

"Not this again!"

He nodded. "I'm afraid so."

I couldn't believe what I was hearing. I'd just climbed one mountain, only to face another.

I took a deep breath and asked if he had to leave home.

Matt explained that Cap had helped him look into enlisting. He would probably be sent to Lowry Field, an air force base in Denver, Colorado.

I couldn't seem to form a response. My mind was swirling. I was angry at being left behind. Then my heart skipped a beat when I realized I might lose him. I took his hand and pressed it to my cheek.

"Are you all right?" he asked.

I wanted to scream no, but what would that accomplish? The truth was, I understood his thinking and would do the same as him if I could. I stood up straight and looked him in the eyes.

"I'll manage. I'll...find something to do here." I had to blink back the tears before they fell. So much for being brave.

Matt wrapped me in a hug and held me for a long time before we continued to the Abernathys'. When we got to the front door, I turned to him.

"When will you be leaving?"

"In a week or two."

I tried to smile as Matt opened the front door. The Abernathys, Elliotts, Mabel's parents, Jack's parents and sisters, and Mr. and Mrs. Baker were all gathered with Mildred in the dining room for our graduation celebration. She had set out a huge selection of sandwiches, desserts, tea, and coffee. I wished my Harbour Grace family could be there too but, according to Mom, Aunt Rose had planned an identical celebration at the hotel. Everyone in town was invited to drop in.

Matt and I filled our plates and joined the others in the living room. We reminisced about our time at Purdue—Professor Jones, Amelia, the football games, the exams, and the flying lessons. Inevitably, the conversation turned to the war.

"Thank goodness the United States is neutral," Mrs. Baker said.

Mr. Baker, Mr. Stinson, Mr. Anderson, and President Elliott stood by the fireplace talking to Professor Abernathy.

"I wouldn't be so sure about that, Helen," Mr. Baker said to his wife. "The professor thinks Roosevelt will help Churchill, the new prime minister, and the Brits any way he can."

"I hope not," Mrs. Stinson cut in. "We're better off staying out of that mess."

I looked at Matt who shook his head slightly. He obviously hadn't told anyone else about his plans.

Mrs. Abernathy steered the conversation to the food Mildred had prepared. We all raved about it and the tone in the room became more relaxed. They told stories about Jamie, Jack, and Mabel growing up. There was laughter and happiness everywhere I looked. But for me, the afternoon dragged on. Everything I put in my mouth turned to clay.

Matt was leaving and I had to stay behind.

CHAPTER 36

GOODBYE

———◀◦▶———

A FTER EVERYONE LEFT the graduation party, Matt and I sat on the swing in the Abernathys' backyard. They had it built the summer before so "the young people" didn't have to sit on the back porch steps. Matt put his arm around me and I looked up at him.

"I'm scared," I admitted.

"I know." He tightened his arm around me. "But I'm not going to be involved in any fighting. Those newsreels made me realize we're lucky to live here, but we can't ignore what's going on in Europe."

I nodded but didn't look up at him in case I burst into tears. We sat for a long time before I asked when he was going to tell his parents.

"When I get home," he replied with a sigh.

"Then I think you should go now, before it gets too late."

"You're probably right. There'll be a lot of discussion about my decision."

I looked up at him and he kissed me. His lips felt soft and warm against mine.

We stood up and followed the gravel path to the front steps where we kissed again. I waited until he got to the corner and waved. I waved back and walked up to the front porch.

I slumped down on one of the chairs and put my face in my hands. What did all of this mean? Would Llewellyn want to join up too? And what about my brother, Billy?

The graduation ceremony was fading and the image of a child sitting next to the body of a dead woman in a potato field in Poland crept in. I pulled myself to my feet and opened the front door. Mildred and the Abernathys were clearing the dining room table when I walked in.

"What lovely people," Mrs. Abernathy said.

I burst out crying and Mrs. Abernathy hurried over to me. She took my hands and led me to the sofa. "What's the matter, my dear?"

When I had stopped crying, Professor Abernathy sat in one of the chairs opposite us. "Is Matt enlisting?"

"How did you know?" I asked.

"I'm afraid it was inevitable."

I sniffed and dried my eyes on my sleeve. "Why do you say that?"

"Matt is a young man with principles. He knows if he can do something to stop that terrible man, he must do it. And don't be surprised if Jack and Jamie do the same thing."

I have principles too, I thought. *Why can't I do something to stop that terrible man?*

"Their poor parents," Mrs. Abernathy said. "What a worry."

Mildred agreed with Mrs. Abernathy and wondered what her sisters' boys would do.

I helped them finish the cleaning up and then walked back to the residence alone. I didn't want to think about what was happening in the Baker household at that moment.

———◦———

A few days later, we all had to move out of residence. Our four years were up and it was time to make room for the summer students. I moved in with the Abernathys to let Mildred spend time with her mother in Alabama. Jack and Ed lived in Lafayette, and the Bakers lived in a town nearby, which meant Mabel was the only one we wouldn't see as often. She lived in Milroy and was not happy about being separated from us.

Matt and I sat on the swing in the Abernathys' backyard, as we did most nights after dinner. The night was warm and the cicadas buzzed loudly. I leaned on his shoulder and he put his arm around me. We sat and watched the sky deepen from orange to red.

"You're awfully quiet," I said after a while.

"My parents got more bad news today. Jamie is enlisting."

I sat up and looked at him. "How are your parents taking it?"

"Not well, I'm afraid. They're worried sick about both of us."

"I'm not surprised. You two are all they have. Have you heard anything about Jack?"

"He's enlisting too."

I sighed and put my head on his shoulder again. "Professor Abernathy said I shouldn't be surprised if you all did."

Matt didn't say anything for a long time. Then he asked if I'd figured out what I was going to do while they were gone.

"I've decided I'll help Cap through the summer. He's looking into some new procedure to help farmers dust their crops. Apparently, it can be done from a plane."

"Sounds like a good idea," Matt replied.

"I wish I could go with you."

He kissed my forehead. "I wish you could too. But the Army Air Corps has rules."

I sighed. "I can fly a crop duster but I can't fly a military plane? Explain that."

"Farmers are more practical than the military," Matt replied. "They don't care who does the job as long as it gets done."

I looked up at him and smiled. "I guess there's no chance of the military getting practical any time soon."

"Not likely," he said.

⊷

Two weeks later, Matt, Jamie, Jack, and Mabel stood with their families at the train station. I wheeled Mrs. Abernathy onto the platform, where Professor Abernathy, Ed, and the Elliotts joined us.

Before we all got there, one more piece of startling news had arrived. Mabel was leaving too. She had enlisted in the US Army Air Corps, just like the boys. With her degree in Home Economics, she'd been offered a job as assistant manager of food services at Langley Field, Virginia. At some point, she hoped she and Jamie could work at the same base.

I felt as if my whole world was boarding the same train. I still had my work at the Abernathys' but no friends to watch movies with and socialize with at the coffee shop. Worse than that, they got to do their part to fight Hitler while I stayed here to dust cornfields.

I looked around the platform and couldn't believe four years had flown by. Although I'd accomplished a lot, I felt the same uncertainty as I had when I first arrived at Purdue. Back then my world was isolated to the train station and the problem of getting to campus. Now my world included a war and all of my friends travelling to far-flung destinations around the country.

Mabel and the boys were dressed in their Sunday best for the journey. We stood around talking quietly and occasionally laughing. Even though the United States was neutral we all knew the political situation around the world was changing daily. No one knew what the future might bring. I wondered if everyone was as scared as me.

From a distance, I heard the train whistle and my heart jumped. We all moved to the edge of the platform. The face of the locomotive grew larger as it got closer. I reached for Matt's hand and squeezed it. The bell started clanging and steam hissed from under the engine before it finally came to a stop.

Mabel dashed over and threw her arms around me. "I can't believe it's been four years since we first stood here and shook hands."

I hugged her back. But before I could say anything, the train whistle blew again. My heart pounded and I felt the same panic as when I'd first arrived. Matt turned to his mom and hugged her tightly and shook hands with his dad. Jamie did the same. I glanced around to see the Andersons and Stinsons doing the same thing.

Mrs. Baker patted Matt's shoulder and wiped a tear from her eye. She turned away as he walked back to me. He hugged me and I held on to him tightly. I wanted to memorize the feeling of his arms around me. I breathed in his scent and kissed his cheek.

"You know I'll be safe, don't you?" he whispered in my ear.

"Yes, but I'll miss you something awful."

"Me too."

Matt took my face in his hands and kissed me on the mouth. Then he stepped back to wave to his parents before he grabbed his knapsack and boarded the train.

Jamie, Jack, and Mabel each hugged me and followed Matt. When they got to their seats, they lowered the windows. I walked over and touched their hands one last time. The bell clanged, the train lurched forward, and I stood back and waved.

I didn't know where or when I would see my friends again—but the tiniest nugget of an idea was forming in my mind.

Amelia and President Edward C. Elliott holding a model of Earhart's "flying labratory" plane, the Electra 10E, in 1936.

L–R: Bo McKneeley, Amelia Earhart, and Captain Aretz in front of Earhart's plane, 1936.

Amelia sitting in the cockpit of her Lockheed Electra.

Amelia (far right) and Fred Noonan (centre) inspecting a fuel drum at Carapito, Venezuela, on June 2, 1937.

AUTHOR'S NOTE

———◀○▶———

AMELIA EARHART WAS employed at Purdue University as a part-time counsellor for women and an aviation advisor from 1935 to 1937. In the fall of 1935 and 1936 her activities were very similar, so I have combined events from both years to give a full picture of her life at Purdue.

ACKNOWLEDGEMENTS

———◦———

I WOULD LIKE to thank those who have assisted in the creation of this book.

Elizabeth A. Hartley, Director of Alumni and Donor Relations, Purdue University, who provided invaluable information about Amelia's time and legacy at the university.

Sammy Morris, University Archivist and Head of Archives and Special Collections Division, Purdue University, who introduced me to the Amelia Earhart Collection; Adriana Harmeyer, Archivist for University History, who offered information and insights into university life in 1936; Neal Harmeyer, Digital Archivist, and Bindu Komalavally, Purdue Research Foundation, who provided the historical photographs; Stephanie Schmitz, Francis A. Cordova Archivist, who helped me locate information in my early days in the library; and David Hovde, Professor Emeritus of Library Science, who provided answers whenever I had questions. The Purdue University Library and its staff couldn't have been more helpful and accommodating.

Kelly Lippi, Curator of Collections, Tippecanoe County Historical Association, who provided early black-and-white photographs of Lafayette, Indiana, and Quentin Robinson, board member and volunteer, who provided detailed local knowledge that allowed me to "see" what lay beyond the photographs.

Bill Rouw, Crew Chief and Flight Engineer on the B-25J Mitchell bomber Hot Gen, Canadian Warplane Heritage Museum, who provided all of the technical aviation information.

Lorraine Brophy, Truus Dragland, Michele Hansen, Roberta Stemp, and Arlene Timmins, of Goderich, Ontario, "first readers" who provided responses to an early version of *Under Amelia's Wing*.

Lexi Harrington, former intern at Nimbus Publishing, who first read *Under Amelia's Wing* (then titled "Taking Flight") and sent it forward.

Whitney Moran, Managing Editor at Nimbus Publishing, who saw value in Ginny's story.

Emily MacKinnon, Editor at Nimbus Publishing, whose suggestions made *Under Amelia's Wing* a stronger book.

My family, Don, James, Jenn, Mike, Sue, Caleb, Maeve, Charlie, and Phaedra, who have provided love and support throughout the life of this book.

HEATHER STEMP'S GRANDFATHER, grand-mother, aunt Ginny, and father Billy were all born and raised in Harbour Grace, Newfoundland. After thirty years as an English teacher, Heather retired and wrote her first book, *Amelia and Me*, which was shortlisted for the 2014/15 Red Cedar Award. *Under Amelia's Wing* is her second book, continuing the story of her aunt's adventures with Amelia Earhart. Heather now lives in North Bay, Ontario, and is working on book three in the Ginny Ross series.